Grassroots Mayhem

David Chamberlain

This goes to Bill who had me laugh so much and is a great friend (One day we will organise the village fete entertainment!).

To Tim a brilliant parent helper who was a great calming influence on the touchline (I love the understated punch!) And who helped analyse my ice cream dream (I am very competitive and have an irrational fear of diary products).

And to all those men and women who give up their time to help the kids play football with their mates.
I salute you and thank you for all your work - the kids love it

CONTENTS

INTRODUCTION

There are over 25000 junior football clubs in England alone. Grassroots football is huge. Every premier player, unless born into a football family, would have started at grassroots clubs before progressing onto Academies and clubs. The club I belonged to had approximately 20 teams including boys and girls teams. With a squad of, say fifteen that is 300 children playing football in our village and catchment area.

All of this is supported by parents, guardians and volunteers, with support from the FA. The parents ferry the children to home and away matches, traning and are hassled for fund raising as well as helping set up.

The volunteers start as too helpful parents that end up picked to volunteer! But must find they like the work and give freely. Some of my most happiest moments are when I am on the side line, the game has started, I am surrounded in beautiful countryside, the sun is shining and 22 kids are having fun with their friends.

This book captures many true moments and observations but in a light hearted way and with genuine respect for all those involved in grassroots football.

I would like to mention the chairman that had given 20 years of his time as a manager and later as chairman and to all the managers in the club. I only think other managers know the anguish we go through!

I would also like to mention the parent helpers. Such a vital and postive force.

I have had to change names to avoid lawsuits and interesting thick letters from solicitor firms but I have had a range of helpers all with their unique style. Jeff who turned up to training in jeans and shoes and promptly left. Simon that spent most of the time roaring with laugher and was brilliant as he did as I asked and was so reliable. He also bought a healthy perscepive to the squad and my expectations. Then there was Tom. Brilliant support - backed me up as the boys got older and more lippy, helped calm me as I tried to sorted out my team sheets with sudden no shows five minutes before kick off and of course his understated competitiveness. The slow punch was a joy to see. And then we get Paul. Who basically was another kid in lyrco shorts and pink top. Reliable and eager but wanting to join in with the squad all the time. I had to drag him out of goal in pre-training to give our goalie a go. He had a roving eye, a potty mouth and an attitude six foot wide. At times I was unable to navigate it and got caught up in situations I would best avoid.

However without any of them the players would not be able to train and play and have as much fun as they did.

This book is dedicated to Saturday and Sunday grassroots across the world - thank you all so much for so much fun!
I salute you all!!

Bill and Me at one of our Respect Tournaments

CHAPTER ONE   AND
SO IT BEGINS

It is the start of the season and looks like it is going to be a hard one. I am standing on the side line watching my team run around like headless chickens. We have just conceded a weak goal that pinged around the six yard box like something out of "Tommy". Our team reverts back to form and I re-assess my ambitions – just not bottom of the table, forget promotion please just not last... It had all started out so well, the pre-season training, the new players, a new training approach from youth module two; where I accept "the chaos"; all gave me a sense of hope, of optimism – which is cruelly crushed within the first ten minutes of play. I look up to the darkening clouds and as the heavens open I think how did it come to this? What on earth am I doing here managing a youth football team at the side of a pitch in the pouring rain, on an early Saturday morning?

This wasn't in my plans, in my life's scheme. I had travelled around the world, surfed in California, Hawaii and New Zealand, seen sunrise over Uluru, danced in Thailand at a full moon party and swam with wild dolphins.

No, nowhere was there "must manage a junior village football team", No, not even in the smallest of small print and believe me I have checked a few times. And then I became a dad and one or two things changed – well actually everything was thrown up in the air and when I made sense of the pieces it made a different life.

And one of those pieces of the jigsaw, one of the best, was the piece that had "play" written on it. And as my son grew the games changed from pulling faces and hiding behind my hands (mmmhm maybe not as he is now learning to drive in my car) to playing football. I don't know where the first football came from but I remember

hanging Jake up in his bouncer from the door way and kicking the ball at him. Hours of fun and therapeutic play for me. And the thoughts started "he's a natural", "look at him kick the ball" and most importantly "he's going to earn me a fortune!"

In the village there was a development football squad – not sure

what that meant – but I took Jake along and so began a fifteen year (and more) relationship with the football club. It all starts off innocent enough - take him up to the fields on Saturday morning, stand around for an hour and go home. Perfect plan - wear the little bugger out and weigh up his earning capacity. Obviously he is a natural and much better than any of the other kids. I don't need to coach him from the side line as the other parents do – he's five years old, of course he knows about the offside rule and through balls. Although some parents advise their children not to pass and keep the ball my son is a generous player and prefers chatting to his mates and running in circles.

The parental one one-upmanship intensifies with each weekend. Maybe I should do some research. Right England are rubbish and need a left footed player – I briefly consider tying his right leg to the chair and get him to pass the ball to me but his mother takes a dim view of this and I opt for playing footie with him in the park – pretty promptly. I continue to take him up to the football club each Saturday – apparently "a dad's job" and he enjoys playing and mixing with his mates. Slowly the manager asks me to help out. First can I put the goal posts out, can I just supervise them for a bit? All innocent enough and I think "Well I'm standing around anyway what harm can it do?" Bad mistake. By March I am helping out on a regular bases – happy doing my civic duty, proud of my increased status from distant spectator dad to helpful dad and then the bomb shell. "Oh we have no one to manager the next age group …can you do it?" Little did I realise that Pete, the developmental coach, had been grooming me all year.

But that was it. Caught – hook line and sinker. What could I say? So I said yes – probably one of the better decisions in my life – though my partner might not quite agree – but one that has given me the most headaches, the most laugh out loud moments and friends I never knew I had. And oh yes and Bob.

CHAPTER TWO   THE
COMMITTEE

Look I'm not stupid. I agreed but I was going to share the job with another parent helper. We were going to manage the next year's team, which only consisted of Saturday morning training. Easy. How hard could it be? So summer came and went and despite the cold sweats and flash backs I was still going to manager the under eights. Lovely age, my son loved nothing better than to run across open space screaming – how hard would fifteen of them be?

Ok what do I need? Kids – check, footballs...no, knowledge of the game – I watch Match of the Day so definitely a check. So I make a few enquiries and find out there is a junior managers meeting. Hey that's me. And then I begin to think – this is quite a bit bigger than I thought. I was vaguely aware of other village teams – I could hear the groans and shouting on Saturdays but it didn't really register. I just thought it was part of village life. So off I go to the meeting – the other manager, Jeff, I am sharing the role with couldn't make it – alarm bells should have sounded then, but no, I sort of give people the benefit of the doubt, but when he turned up for training in shoes and jeans ten minutes late a blue light somewhere should have gone off.

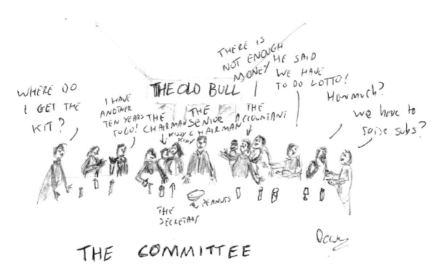

THE COMMITTEE

The meeting is traditionally held in the pub – good start but we quickly go upstairs and sit round a table where there is an air of sullen expectation. The chairman, accountant and the junior chairman enter and the meeting begins. Straight down the list – where are the subs? Managers named and shamed, what the plans for the future are – massive flood lit training ground, volunteers needed to raise money and then some more money – we all on cue become interested in the inside of our pints and then any other business. Well yes – I'm the new manager who is everybody but more importantly

"Where do I get footballs?"

"In the lock up"

"How do I get in the lock up?"

"You need a key"

"Can I have a key?"

"We don't have any available"

"How do I get kit?"

"You get sponsorship"

"Who from?"

"The parents"

So with no keys available I had to run in and out on Saturday morning whilst the "lock up" was unlocked. It took me two years to get the keys which I promptly lost. And that's when I also encountered the right of passage. Kit. All managers got sponsorship from their parents – or more commonly from their company. Me being a NHS librarian – I could just about muster a pen and some post-it notes but home and away kit and training kits and coats – there are some wealthy company directors on the committee. Or to be fair – self-employed tax evaders! Right so self-sponsorship out the parents are paying subs, we have to get them to sign up to money making schemes (astro-turf and lotto) and then get one poor sucker to pay for the kit. I mean did I join a football club or a fund raising charity? I leave straight after the meeting understanding the sullen faces a bit more. And with no key or kit.

First training day is fast approaching and I think my knowledge gleaned from Match of the Day might not be enough. I have no real experience of football as a boy to call on. It was all cricket and rugby apart from the 5 aside club where I was promptly put in goal and stayed there for most of the year. Unfortunately I was that kid who got picked last. Oh well, being a librarian I had a book and a plan. A plan to make training plans. Yes that was good, bits of paper.

So armed with footballs (of a mixed variety) and bits of paper I was nearly ready. All I needed was to look the part. So what better than to wear your premier team shirt (from a couple of seasons ago mind you, as have you seen the price they charge? I mean we are advertising their club they should at least pay us….or make it a reasonable price). Anyway – team shirt it is - bad, bad mistake.

The first day dawns, I'm up and ready and Jeff arrives late in jeans and says "What you going to do then?" Not even a we, but a you – alarm bells! And then the kids turn up and spot the premier shirt and all hell breaks loss – "what you wearing that for?" Why don't you support a local team?" "My team thrashes your team" and on and on until I realise distraction is the best method and point at a goal and shout "let's run to it" phew 10 seconds to re-think as Jeff just grins at me.

I set up a passing game that goes reasonably well and soon work out that long drawn out discussion on tactics and explanation of complex drills is not needed. A short sharp drill followed by a match seems to be the order of the day. When I say match there is of course an assumption of a pitch with boundaries, positions, rules, goalkeepers some form of game plan. I use the word match without any of those assumptions. Please try and imagine sixteen little kids running around after a ball kicking it as hard as they can and very often completely missing whilst their parents shout positional advice from the side lines. At least they haven't started chanting about the coach. So the first day goes well and develops into a fairly set routine.

With only training on Saturdays and no matches with other clubs there was little pressure, so ditching the football shirt and keeping the training plans the first season quickly passed. But still no kit. My life remained fairly normal- football only on Saturdays at term times (oh the happy ignorant bliss!), no matches or training to arrange and only small goals to hump back and forth from the other lock up – the dreaded green container, conveniently situated at the furthest point from any playing pitches and covered in rust.

But all this was to change. Next season we join a league and I have to get my coaching badge.

CHAPTER THREE
GETTING BADGED UP

Right the pressure from the committee is on – get a coaching qualification and get a kit. Still no keys and none of my parents have signed up for the astroturf super lotto direct debit bingo yet. I have sent an e-mail out into the void asking for sponsorship but strangely I have not had a reply. The accountant continues to glare at me and reads out all those who have signed up to the astro-turf lotto thing, noticeably the chairman's, the accountant's and junior chairman's teams. The other managers all study the floor. Jeff turns up late and promptly volunteers us both to do the coach training. Nice one. The committee all seem pleased and I have a sense of impending doom as all the other managers start retelling tales of their training and start talking in a language vaguely familiar to me – drills, tactics, off-side. But at least Jeff is going with me and we have safety in numbers i.e. I can hide behind him. So, I sign up on line and take the plunge.

Oh dear Jeff can't make the dates I choose but will sign up for the next one – alarm bells. Committed (I should be) I go to the first aid course and safe guarding. Spend most of the time fretting about what to wear at the first aid – shorts? Too creepy. Jeans? Too uncomfortable, tracksuit? Probably the best but I feel a complete idiot – like I have gone out in my pyjamas.

Oh well mouth to mouth with a plastic manikin might be considered fun in some areas of Soho but we all endure three hours and flee. Safe guarding isn't much better, but at least I don't have to roll around on the floor. However for some reason  the training is a little hostile as the coaches drill the trainer with worse case scenarios – "What do you do if the parents haven't turned up, there is only you and it is pouring with rain and it is getting dark? Do you let the child sit in your car and accuse you of child molestation? Or watch the child die of pneumonia whilst you sit in your car? They might as well have included the prince of darkness and Rolf Harris and given you a Jim'll fix it badge at the end!

And then things go a bit bizarre. One of the scenarios is a child that turns up for training with smack marks and our table conclude he probably deserved it! And then there is a debate on who hasn't smacked their child. Apparently this isn't a black and white area – more black and blue. On leaving one man angrily decries that the world has gone mad with too many safety checks (he probably at some stage said "PC gone mad" and "I blame the EU"), but I point out that all we had to do is contact a welfare officer if we were unsure – but it falls on deaf ears and I leave a sadder but wiser man.

The weekend arrives for first level training and I have invested in a new track suit bottom – no matching top and definitely not a woolly one. I also go out and buy myself a pair of football boots. The first pair in thirty years! Haven't changed much – go for the cheap hobnailed clogs at the back and avoid the bladed colourful ballet type strength slippers at the front. I read all the pre-course stuff and buy a new note pad - ready.

The room is full of young adults, a few grizzled types that wouldn't look out of place cage fighting and one or two keen teenagers. And oh yes - one middle aged dad who feels completely out of place. No females of course, ethnic minorities or gay footballers, yes it is macho alpha football. The young university students want to train at academy's and seem to have the perfect squad and the ex-Sunday footballers, with injuries to horrendous to list, want to pass on their ancient knowledge and craft – which mainly consists of swearing and "letting 'em have it!". No one seems to be a dad, picked to volunteer to coach a team of hyperactive children of mixed ability. Ok that is not fair – degraded children with below average ability and a clueless coach that means well.

But no worries – we are here to learn by doing – out on the pitch for drill after drill – the grizzled types go in goal or watch the carnage, the younger men dance round with the ball and I feel like that guy who hoofs it in the beer ad. Pecking order very swiftly determined by ability – school flash back becomes a reality as I'm picked last. But blow that, I am here to learn and volunteer for each drill. My fitness keeps me going – all those years of running – and I last the first day.

The second day is more of the same – hardly able to move (oh the vanity of a fairly fit man) I decide to alternate volunteering for drills, seemingly to the relief of the academy coaches – who in my opinion are taking this a bit too seriously. The drills are interspersed with discussion as we debate whether anyone can actually learn or are they already talented. Why are the children there? I have often asked my partner the same question. And what style of coaching can we/ should we use – no one laughs at my young Mr Grace approach to management joke " You have all done very well!" as I suspect the majority were not even born when the series was on TV.

At the end of Sunday we are all given our drills to do for the assessment. I have "See it, do it". One of my favourites throughout the years as it turns out, as it is a deceptively simple drill involving space, decision making and passing. I say deceptively simple as it certainly fooled all my

squad. Back at normal training with my squad of under eights I practice this drill. The chaos this caused was unbelievable. Firstly no one listened, secondly, three boys broke into a fight, thirdly no one knew what space was and fourthly they had no concept of passing. However they all agreed to not listen so that showed some degree of unity... right? Alright a third level degree but a degree nevertheless!

In fact half way through the drill when I was yelling (oops encouraging) our players to move into space one boy asked what space was. I had images of him imagining me telling him to go into outer space and wondering for half the drill why I wanted him to do that and how he was to achieve it.

After this rather stressful training session I suddenly realised I was going to breeze the assessment and what was fundamentally wrong with the course. At the weekend we had all listened to the explanations of the drills, asked questions and tried our hardest to follow the instructions. No one was watching the clouds or kicking a football or shoving each other and fighting – we were all adults. If I could get my lot to follow half the drill doing it with adults would be easy.

And so with a Saturday for practising the assessments followed on the Sunday. We nearly all passed except for one manager who decided to merge two drills into one and bizarrely asked the players to call themselves girl's names to encourage passing.

I got through and earned a level 1 FA football coaching badge. How strange was that? And then as the new season starts Jeff announces he is not going to continue and I am left to manage the training and matches alone. I did not see that one coming but apparently Jeff did.

CHAPTER FOUR THE PLAYERS AND INJURIES

The players. Where would we be without them? Probably at home in bed having a second cup of tea. Sometimes I look at my lot and just shake my head. The anguish and

the joys they have put me through. As a dad I cannot think of a greater joy than watching my sons play football, with big grins on their faces, chatting with their mates in a lovely park or countryside and even throw in a bit of football skill and the odd goal. But to manage them. Now that's different.

This season I was on my own and

had not only training to manage but we were in a league with home and away matches. I had to assess my player's capabilities.

Let's think about their technical ability with the ball. Obviously that varies for every child and varies throughout their playing development. It also varies within a nano second on the pitch – a brilliant one two is followed by a missed hoof that sees the opposing team perform a brilliant counter movement. And then the decision to try a piece of technical skill, although always welcome, might not always be timed right when on the edge of the box, my player decides to dribble the ball out and throw in a couple of step overs and turns as well and then promptly loses the ball. I thought I liked the passing game but I slowly found myself on the "get rid of it" side of the philosophical debate. Incidentally that attitude has come back to haunt me as now I beg the defenders to pass the ball out of defence instead of booting it straight at their midfield to be on the receiving end of yet another counter attack. The last game was a cross between the Alamo, shooting fish in a barrel and ten pin bowling – and we were the pins.

Looking at their physical strength, the child and the squad will vary and the trick of the coach is to try and match up the whole team so they balance out. That does not mean the tallest in goal and the small fast ones up front, although this has seemed to happen in my squad – strange that. Although my tall goal keeper compensates for the advantage of his height by refusing to dive. We might be playing in conditions that war veterans at the Somme might just give up and shake hands and go home but he would come off in pristine condition his knees glowing white relaxed and unflustered as though he had been on a Sunday morning stroll in the park.

PLAYING "THE SOMME" PITCH

In fact, he is one of the most nonchalant relaxed players I have ever seen. Casually putting a hand or a foot out here or there, picking the ball out from the back of the net as though it is a bit of lint on his Sunday blazer. A cheery wave and a smile, not a care in the world. I spend most of my time just shaking my head in disbelief.

Football is also a physical game, oh yes a rugby player is hard as nails and can run through a brick wall – yes we know that. In fact a coach to my oldest son e-mailed all the parents with a story how a rugby player had crushed one of his testicles and still carried on playing. It was a gruesome read but the point of the example was how he wanted his squad of ten year olds to be committed and "show some balls". Unfortunately mine are all polite gentleman "No after you I insist" and we get roughed up by an age group below us in a friendly and we come off genuinely surprised and shocked.

One of the main aspects for the players is the social side of the game. Even if it might not be with another human being. George spent one game running round the pitch and tackling with a mud ball in his hand and only let go of it after being threatened to be substituted. Another player pretended to be a chicken for a game and in fact recruited the opposition into doing a chicken dance during the after match hand shake. Whilst one match a players pet dog ran on to the pitch, which in itself isn't too bad, but it was tied to a plastic garden chair. It took three parents, the referee and a linesman to catch it and the game descended into chaos with whooping children.

Of course there is the other side to this coin – anti-social behaviour. Feuds from school often surface during training and matches despite the "we are a team and we win together and lose together" approach. One match my defence not only were refusing to talk to each other but refusing to pass. We held on for the first half and despite a half time team talk that bordered on hysterical pleading, like some mafia feud, the hostilities continued.

And then we have the psychology of our players - my favourite bit – thinking football. This is a dream when it starts happening. For years it's been set positions; defenders on guard on the edge of the box, midfield trying to be strikers, striker's goal hanging and then suddenly one player starts to think about football. A through ball, running off the ball, a drop of a shoulder and a one two – lovely to see and watch. But rare, these are moments to enjoy, to look back on, the running at the defence and the passing and shot in the top left hand corner – lovely football. But to get there, there are hours spent sitting down with a board explaining positions and movement, of trying to be heard above the general noise of arguments, back chat and loaded opinions of player ability. And then there is the on the pitch concentration. One player had particular difficulties in remaining focused so I made him captain in the hope that that might help. At the end of the game as the players lined up to shake hands the captain was not to be found, but was down the other end of the pitch watching another game. He had to be told that our match had finished.

And of course there is the handling of the players own expectations and the pressure they feel under from their parents and friends. We have a laurel bush that separates the tennis courts from the football pitches – a sort of posh divide that has become a refuge for players. One lad after a poor performance in goal took shelter in the dense growth and had to be coaxed out during a game muttering about his "shame". However this set precedence and another striker fled the pitch to find solace amongst the laurel bushes only for his dad to go in after him and whilst we all stood on the pitch we could hear the psychology

"You get back on that f-ing pitch, where's your f-ing balls!!?"

"I'm going to cut them off if you don't get back on there!?"

What is it with balls and psychology? But it worked. The player came back on as we all stood there in embarrassed silence relieved to continue the game.

And then there are injuries and the feigned injuries! So, last game of the season, just managed to get a squad together with no substitutes for a grudge match. Unfortunately it's my grudge as the other manager bellows at his team and their supporters whoop with delight with each goal they score. Anyway waiting for the last player to turn up for a lift and I get a text "Johnnie isn't feeling well and can't make it" He is home alone so I offer to see if he is alright. He refuses to answer the door and I leave late for the match one player down and have to play against a team that put out a full squad against our reduced team. We hold on for a bit but concede weak goals to the squealing delight of their fans. Johnnie later decides to leave the team for another team "because I am fed up with losing" and I wish him well through clenched teeth.

The real injuries on the pitch aren't really dealt with in the first aid training. We do not often get heart attacks and deaths more the cuts and bruises injuries. But occasionally we have a few broken legs. Unfortunately both my sons have broken something during football. The first break was when my eldest broke his leg as he and another player hit the ball at the same time. The ball remained stationary so I suppose the energy had to go somewhere (thank you Mr Young for my o level physics!). Unfortunately the manager was that "play with crushed balls e-mailer" and as Arthur was carried off he suggested he walk it off and get back on. As luck would have it an A & E doctor was watching his son and made a prompt diagnosis and we spent my birthday in hospital. The other injury was to my second son, forget his name (you know how it is with the second one..) and we were having

a friendly (again with a grudge team but this time the grudge was with my squad as I quite liked their manager – rarity that). Anyway my son begs to go in goal, so I thought "Why not he is the manager's son" so he went in and in the first attack he comes out one on one and crashes straight into their striker and seriously damages his knee. Fortunately his screams of agony help me make a decision and off he goes to A & E and again almost uncannily near my birthday again. The little buggers do it on purpose. He eventually gets a diagnosis and is operated on a couple of days later and we limp to the end of the season, literally.

As the squad gets older I have to watch for growth spurts and ensure the boys are warmed up and down properly with stretches and exercises. However this season I have been plagued by football and non-football injuries.

One player hurt his foot in training and his mum held him off football for 2 months for him to then hurt his finger in goal on his return to be off for a further month. Another player drops an alloy on his foot and we see nothing of him or his monthly subscriptions – just vanished off the face of the earth. And then our goal keeper grows even more and his muscles can't keep up and his is off sport for six months at least. OK no worries put our second goalie in – we lose him from defence but we have a good line up. He then goes and breaks his arm in rugby – previously in the season he broke his collar bone – a mad bicycle trick on the playing fields. OK we have a third goalie – a bit rusty but he was our second choice last year. We are riding high in the table and I begin to have delusions of grandeur. We could get promotion here. Right one training session to go before vital match and I decide to work our third keeper to get him up to scratch. But he does not turn up for training – I text his mum and apparently his Dad fell asleep on the sofa and Sam takes advantage to play x-box and could not walk the 400m to the village playing field. I am incensed. How can he not turn up to training? Can't he walk? I offer to do one to one goal keeping with him and my son the next evening – yes, like I really want to do this and, I think, he is forced to attend. I manage a few catching and diving drills and notice he has a tendency to use his feet rather than his hands. I encourage him to remember he is a keeper and pray to the football gods.

Who obviously prefer to have a laugh as on match day he refuses to use his hands and within the first ten minutes concedes three easy catches by tapping a slow rolling ball out to on coming forwards who smash it home. Three nil and game over. My defence then decide to protect the keeper and remain in defence when we attack and play everyone on side. My forwards, with nowhere to go, lose the ball and it is dinked over the midfield into about fifty yards of space. Their forwards come straight at us but no, our defenders twenty yards away see what is happening and run full speed out of defence to win the ball and kick it out to kingdom come...but no the forward dribbles it round the rushing defender whose momentum takes him to the other side of the sodding pitch as he air kicks the vanished ball and it is three on one with my keeper who decides to stay on his line and save with his feet!! I hold my head in my hands and mutter dark and terrible curses.

So next game out he comes and our fourth goal keeper goes in – he previously played in goal for another team before joining us but turns out to be an excellent defender. And suddenly my season implodes as I have a fourth choice goal keeper and lose two important defenders. My game plan boils down to hoof the ball up front and score more goals than the opposition and we win. Unfortunately that only worked once and we slide down the table ending not with a bang, but a whimper.

Our team injury sheet this season consisted of knee misalignment, broken foot, broken arm, sprained ankles, suspected fractured foot, suspected fractured finger and broken collar bone. Wenger would be pleased with that list.

CHAPTER FIVE   THE EQUIPMENT AND MARKING OUT

OK – I've got the kids, I have been to the committee meetings but I need the stuff to play football with. To start with we have the lock up – a broom cupboard sized room attached to the sports hall which is owned by the bowling club and the senior football club i.e. out of bounds, and we have the green container; a sort of elephants grave yard of plastic football goals.

With a key to the lock up I rummage around and find several disregarded kits that I mix up for our squad. We might resemble a joint casting of Oliver and South Pacific (the kit is bright yellow and blue and of varying sizes) but at least we look like a team. I hit the jack point and find some new footballs of the right size, some bibs and cones. To my eternal shame I remember once just before a match one of the opposing academy ambitious coaches trying to engage me in football talk and asked me "How I found the new premier footballs?" I replied "oh in the lock up" and only realised my social faux pas after the match – he was asking about their weight and flight. Well it explained the look. The club supplies a first aid kit and I seriously worry about some of the injuries I might encounter – there is a splint, slings, enough bandages for a mummy, ice packs, tin foil blankets and vials of water (I assume). However no plasters or wipes, which in my experience are the two main things I spend my time looking for. The club also provides drink canisters and a carrier.

Right so when I leave the car and try and find the football pitch – I am talking about playing away here and not at

home – my parking isn't that bad, I am carrying a bag of 14 footballs, a first aid kit, 8 drink canisters and a sports bag containing bibs, cones, match ball, white board and pens, forms, rule book and player ids. The players have run off to the swings and the parents are late. I look like some bag lady snail man and stagger towards the fields.

At home it isn't much better. To start with the goals were plastic tube relics that were easy enough to carry but difficult to match up as they were all broken and mismatched. The club in my second year bought new metal goals with three different sizes and with metal hinged sides. These also came with a large metal pole to secure the hinges with pins (quickly lost) and two large weights to secure the poles. They looked really smart but heavy to carry. Unfortunately the green container was four hundred metres away from where we played.

This meant, with a helper, four trips back and forth from the green container just to set up; first carrying one goal, then the other, then two sets of weights each and then two poles. The flags and the respect barrier were kept separately in the lock up. That could be done in one trip. So for a match you ask the opposition and our players to turn up half hour early so they could warm up. You arrive an hour early to start to set up.

Of course no parent arrives that early, despite asking, so you set up the flags, respect barrier, get the weights out and the poles. Parents turn up at the same time as the referee, your players and the opposition. So you try to welcome the away coach, pay and chat to the referee, finish off setting up and get your players warmed up after you have collected all the balls they have just helped themselves to and kicked like atoms around the pitch.

And once the match is done – the next game is to try and grab a parent before they disappear to put the whole lot back again.

The routine for the goals is also the same for a training session sans officials but with the added excitement of competing for your ground. Matches are allocated to set pitches. We now play on the senior flat pitches but on pain of death are not allowed to train on them. This gives us "the swamp" or "the slope" options with everyone else. Obviously times and days are not coordinated and on Thursdays at 6pm (the most popular time) the fields resemble "It's a knockout" as we try and set up before anyone else and stake out our claim.

One of the many rites of passages that I happy volunteer for as I am too slow to step back with the rest of the managers is the marking out of the pitches. So with the junior chairman and his very amorous dog I help out marking the pitches with a spray can, a paint coated measuring tape and a proto type machine for pouring paint onto the pitch having first blocked itself gurgled, dribbled and then turned into a dead weight. Being apprentice I had the tape measure and spray can. The responsibility was heady as I tried to work out squares, divisions, circles and penalty spots all in straight square angles. But despite the Heathcliff moments with the dog on the wind swept pitches we managed well and I was ready to go alone. Unfortunately that included Bob.

Apparently he had been marking out pitches all season and when the chairman sent one of his "despairing lack of help, he's too busy, the pitches aren't marked, I'm going to kill all the managers and I have had enough" e-mails Bob and I decided to step up to the mark – OK we were the only ones to answer his e-mail. So I was busy measuring the pitch that Bob had already marked out and he asked me what I was doing with the measuring tape. So I told him

And he says "Oh I do it by eye".

"Well that explains why this pitch is three metres narrower at one end!".

"Oh never mind – we can use the smaller goal for that end and put it in perspective!"

I find out the real reason why the angles go a bit off. Later as I chat to him as he is marking out by "eye" next to the tennis courts he notices the female team playing and I realise the angle of pitch begins to veer to the tennis courts as his "eye" goes off course.

CHAPTER SIX   TOXIC
PARENTS

Where on earth do you start with the parents? Possibly herding them over the edge of a cliff, dumping them off into the Antarctic with Bear Grylls or smile manically and listen to them spout the bloody obvious. I had one come up to me today after a training session (after we lost a tight match – both sides were rubbish, we were just rubbish more often!) and he said I think we need to work on passing "Of course we need to work on passing and while we're at it we need to working on defending, goalkeeping, attacking, set pieces, throw ins you name it we need to work on it!!" I have one hour with the players – what does he think I can do in that time? But at least the well-meaning parent can be directed to the dreaded green container for some goal post humping.

It is the aggressive parent that are the worse. The one who expects you to turn their mildly talented son into a premier super star and blames you if they are not whisked off to the Emirates (OK I'm biased) old Trafford (oops sorry past glory days) Stamford bridge then (oh dear what a season) must be King Power ground in a limousine. They are also the ones who don't lift a finger or offer any help and stand solitary on the side lines shouting singular advice and glaring at you. I suppose it didn't bode well when in a training session I was momently distracted as I was helping another player who had hurt themselves, and of course having no helpers the players were left to their own devices. One player (the mud ball kid) kicked the ball into a pack of unaware players. His son got the ball full in the face.

After the training when you are surrounded by children and parents all telling you so and so can't make the match, where is the match, how do I pay the subs, the dad comes marching up shouting "You can't control your players!!" Note not our children – but your players. I thought he was joking so I agree with him "Of course I can't" I mean there is no point in denying it one adult versus fifteen kids – and mark out the pitch, carry the goals, set up the drills, deliver the training, administer first aid and maintain discipline – ha! All the other parents at this stage shuffle to the background as he continues to shout and I realise he is being serious as I watch his mouth bark up and down. I remain calm and state I need help (I reflect, of a psychiatric kind as I put up with this nonsense). And he storms off.

He continues to stalk the side line during matches but the parents rally and Simon volunteers to help me. A great giant of a man that laughs at everything – but mostly at the football – and brings a welcome light relief and I reflect, some muscle. He also brings a sponsor and for the first time we have matching kit and not a rag assortment of old kit from the lock up. However things come to a head when during a match I advise Alex to watch the offside when he is in his own half (oh heinous of crimes) and his father starts to bellow "You don't know the rules" over and over again.

I place my fingers to my lips in a sssh gesture and indicate with my other hand raised that he is talking in an attempt to get him to be quiet but I realise from his position across the field it looks like I am doing a Hitler nazi salute and he becomes incensed. He threatens all manner of punishment and dire consequences accumulating in removing his son from the club. Fortunately

his wife had a quiet word with him and he received a touch line ban and his son continued to play the football he loved. In fact he played better without his dad's menacing presence.

Another type of parent is the one that thinks you are offering a Saturday morning crèche while they stay at home. I mean I can understand having to go to work but to stay at home and chose not to watch your son? Weird. Very occasionally they might wander by with the dog but absolutely nothing. Just a convenient crèche service that involves football. This type of parent is one of the ones most hated by any managers. To hear them at the committee meetings all crèche parents would suffer every diabolical pain conceived in the hell realms. I think the hatred stems from the contrast of time and effort all the volunteer managers put in with that kind of parent. As the rain lashes down and you are soaked to the skin humping those goals towards the green container evil thoughts just seem to come naturally to you.

But, I think the ideal parent would be the one that pays all their subs on time, appear miraculously when you need the goals to be put out and then retreat to the side-line to give encouraging support to the players. They then, without coercing put the goals away at the end of the match, never show at training and buy you a box of chocolates (anything Cadburys – very serious hint) at the end of the season. Instead I get deranged yelling parents, if they show at all, that not only scream at me but shout criticising comments not only at our own players but their own son and then have to be marched at gun point to help out.

This season I have come across a new parent – the worried mum. It seems to be a bit of a disorder – the first stage is the "Why is my son in defence? He should be up front". This manifests in comments and asides. Then follows the "no one is passing to him" and the "Everyone says he's rubbish" phase that comes in waves of texts. And then finally paranoia sets in "He's going to be dropped" "He's subbed more than anyone else" that no amount of explanation or reassurance seems to help. Meanwhile the player blissfully plays his game.

However the one uncanny ability any parent has is that they can disappear within a split second, usually after a match or a training session. Normally I am surrounded at the end of each session with parents and players asking questions, giving me kit sizes, wanting times, directions and I am trying to collect bibs, footballs, water containers, ensure all the kids are being picked up and before I know it, after packing the bibs away I look up and the pitch is deserted. The goals all up, the flags standing and the respect barrier in place. And I begin to lug them all back to the green container.

And then it gets dark and starts to rain and as I drag one of the goals I trip over the other goal and momentarily I am trapped on the floor between two goals in the pouring ran like a wet fish and I think about parentcide.

Ok it's not all doom and gloom. We did have one young mum help out with the goal posts and then from nowhere dads came out of the hedges and fields to fall over themselves to lift the goal posts with her. I seriously have never seen so many men run across the playing fields nor so many holding on to a goal. The pitch was cleared in seconds.

And then this season we have a first: opposition parents. And if I thought our parents were bad, the opposition's are even worse. Loud, noisy and worse of all jeering and laughing at our lads. A tight game is always exciting and you would expect oohs and ahhs but when you are on a receiving end of a one sided score the jubilant laughs and celebrations of the opposition parents is enough to send a manager over the edge "Come on Jimmy get a hat-trick… like everyone else – ha ha" - "Yeah come on Jimmy I dare you!!" and then he does. And our parents start joining in and criticising our players "Oh Charlie" rings out and I ask the ref how long to go… twenty minutes…a life time. I glare darkly at the parents opposite but they are too busy laughing and drink coffee. I sigh despairingly.

CHAPTER SEVEN   THE TEENAGER IN BLACK

To begin with for the first two seasons the referees are the coaches or a well-meaning parent. This is completely fraught with issues and problems. So many tackles go unchallenged that a match often turns into an ugly WWE session or the re-creation of the battle of pearl harbour by the Batley Townswomen Guild. My players come off incensed and small grudges develop. This gets so bad that on one occasion a player punches another during the respect handshake. I was at accident and emergency at the time as my son had broken his leg at the same match! We really should be sponsored by air ambulance.

Many coaches are unable to adapt to the neutral aspect of their role as referee and continue to coach their team during the game. Impotent at the side line I break all rules and shout at the referee to no avail. But at least the coach knows the rules. When the referee is a well-meaning parent the rules become subjective and the match resembles a Sunday kick around in the park. This normally wouldn't matter too much but at the same time as referees are introduced so is a league table.

Ah the league tables- the complete bane of my life that fuels all my attempts at suppressing my competitiveness. The games are now more serious; parents monitor the league positions and give you helpful reminders of where you are in the table (bottom end) and the consequences of a loss. And in truth I watch them in some masochistic macabre post-match dread that would make any self-flagellating Swede proud. I hate league tables.

As the boys get older the league starts to appoint trained referees to the games. These vary from trainee young lads to old stalwarts imparting their knowledge; who pedantically line up the kids and give them a speech about what they will and will not allow to happen on the pitch…football seems to be the main casualty.

But in all fairness I have no idea why anyone would want to be a referee. My niece upon going to her first premiership match informs me she has learnt that the referee is a w**ker. And to be honest the abuse and swearing at these matches is embarrassing. Although none of this swearing has passed down to grass roots, the ref still seems to be where all the frustration is directed and cannot be a comfortable place.

In one grass roots cup final the referee had to call the police as the parents started fighting after a tackle between two players. And in a local league game where my son was playing a parent offered to take out a seventy-two year old grandfather as tempers flared. And as for the swearing amongst the players as they get older – under fifteens and sixteens – it would make a navvy blush.

Recently I instigated putting up outdoor displays saying " Welcome, please remember the coaches are volunteers, the players are children and the referees are only human – playing with respect" . Somebody ran it over. Probably Bob, as he in all seriousness told me that if his team is being "roughed up a bit" he gets his players in a match to kick the ball at the opponents as hard as they could. This year his team won the league fair play award. Am I on the same planet as everyone else?

CHAPTER EIGHT   OTHER CLUBS

With the league, gone are the days of playing friendlies and having a laugh, now it is the serious business of thrashing kids from weird villages – Upper Bottomly, Wyre Piddle (real name) and other Viking/Saxon names – Kirby Muxloe. So it's on the blower to arrange home and away matches.

Oh the joys of away matches – long drives to muddy fields, with no facilities, two plastic goals (probably bought from Argos) and a dozen psycho parents leering at you like something out of "Deliverance".

I'm sure I hear banjos playing as we traipse off the undulating field and try to navigate our way home. I refuse to use a sat. nav. and end up having to cross a river. We live in England for heaven's sake. And then with a car load of kids, yes the old "Can you give my son a lift?" times four I have a great responsibility to control my road rage. This all goes wrong when in a tight right hand turn out of the village I accidentally cut in front of a land rover who proceeds to tail gate me and blast their horn. They overtake on a straight and I follow shouting obscenities and giving them a none too friendly hand gesture before I realise I have a car load of silent kids. My partner didn't speak to me for a week – the one and only time she has offered to help and I blow it.

Our home pitches aren't much better, we have "the slope" and "the swamp". Both challenging in their unique way but at least we have facilities, the laurel bush next to the tennis club. One nil to class war.

Strangely enough every season I seem to have a grudge team. A team that winds me up so much that I implore all the gods to strike them down with a thrashing only to be thwarted by cruel fate and left like Wenger at Stamford Bridge. A team I watch rise up in the league tables as my team falls like some soul tied to a medieval wheel of fortune.

The first season it was Muxloe. Fresh from my coach training I had the assumption that a coach encourages from the side-line and offers positive support. The Muxloe manager screamed the whole time from kick off to final whistle yelling where players should be, what they should do and whether they played well (apparently not very often) or badly (most of the time). I couldn't get a word in and at one stage thought he was going to have a heart attack his face had turned so red. We lost that one, but our match at home we drew – first point of the season! He did however continue his diatribe of constant screaming and being devil's advocate I listened to his after match team talk.

"That team was rubbish and haven't won anything and you couldn't even beat them – I haven't come here to waste my Saturdays to see you do squat diddly-dee"

Stirring stuff – off my Christmas card list but on my list of hate – just above the green container.

There are always a few managers that shout negative comments throughout the match but the ones that really get me are the ones that field a full squad against your depleted squad. We have always struggled to get a full squad and at the start of the last two seasons we were down by a player. So you talk to the manager say you haven't got a full squad "Oh that doesn't matter" and when you turn up to play he fields nine (plus four subs) against your eight. And we hold on for half a match but end up with a cricket score. And when I say this isn't fair the response?

RIVAL MANAGERS

"I want to win"

Great good on you – those stupid league tables and competitive managers.

And when I kept shouting encouragement to my boys "Come on lads its nine versus eight" their manager had the audacity to ask me to stop mentioning the squad size. Well he's on my list too.

At the end of each week we write our match reports for our website.

This is what I actually wrote:

Match report 20th December Bridlington 5 vs 3 Westbury

A cold wet morning with us all thinking of Christmas holidays. The game was over by half time and the highlight was Alex's goal in the second half that was a lightening shot from the edge of the box after some lovely control. The team did not give up and we continued to push throughout the game. Tom in particular fought hard in midfield".

However this is what I would have liked to have written:

"Spineless s**ts Bridlington so desperate for a win put out 9 players against 8 aside Westbury who are down to 8 'cos s**t Joe pretends to be sick so he can play f**king x-box whilst his home alone parents play horsey horsey in Kidderminster and despite the s**ts at Bridlington we took the game to them and nearly drew but lost to the unsporting f**k team 5-3 and even the ref shook our players hands but that doesn't change the fact that s**t managers are going to f**king burn in HELL!!!!"

Whilst the former report went on the website the latter report is much more accurate and interesting but totally illegal. Although Bob did threaten to post it and it has cost me a few beers post season de-brief

CHAPTER NINE COPING WITH COMPETITIVENESS

I do a lot of meditation and running, I can meditate for an hour and run 20k. I have done mud runs, fun runs, gone into retreats but none of it has an actual effect on my competitiveness. I want to win and beat every team mercilessly. I want the competition to be over within the first ten minutes – in our favour for once, and I want to win a trophy…just one – a bloody big one.

But then I manage a group of village boys who are all mates and enjoy football. And really that is what I want to nurture. We have a couple of boys all of a mixed skill base and a couple with some mild form of disability. And after each match, despite the score, they are to be found with the opposition players mucking about on the swings or climbing frames. The match forgotten and the current moment enjoyed. And so the managers have to hold them-selves in check, but every so often, once or twice, it might burst out.

I know one manager (yes lets name names – Bob) when his team scored he ran half way down the pitch did a Mourihno type dive on his knees cheering. It wouldn't have been so bad but it wasn't even a winner – just an equaliser. He can still remember that silent walk back to the touchline and the open mouth stare of the other manager.

The same manager, when winning, subs his players from the furthest end of the pitch and gets them to walk back to the touch line to waste time. And once during a respect tournament he primed his parents to cheer the opposition if they scored and make loud encouraging comments so they might win the respect trophy – which they dually did! Bob – how can you live with yourself?

There are coaches who instruct their players to stand in front of the goalie and to man mark, all perfectly legal but in a game with eight year olds? We conceded a goal once where the opposition had a direct free kick, their players in the wall pushed our line apart and they shot and scored through the gap. I had to applaud that one but wish we had done it.

And I think that is the problem. All the managers want to win and right from the start at the training for our badges the coaches talk as if they have premiership players and discuss tactics and ability as though their players are going on to play for the top teams, but we are a village league with young children wanting a kick around. And the frustration is you have one hour a week of training and a complete mix of different skilled players and you must weigh that against your own competitiveness.

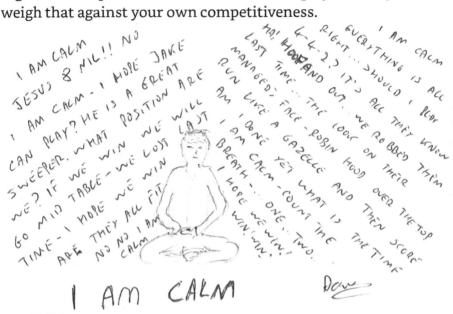

However as the boys get older the competitiveness comes into their game. The ref is biased, that player is winding them up, one of their own players is weak, it all intensifies and I have to try and get them to see that they play as a team and respond to "unfairness" by upping their game. Yeah as though that has ever worked! But one of the best feelings is when you are playing a top team and their manager is all smiles and politeness as he assumes the three points are his. And then you beat them and he has to carry on that level of politeness but he is seething inside and just wants to yell at the players (oops bit of transference there!). We had an under sixteen game recently and played a team we have never played before who was fighting for top spot. I had done my usual optimism slide with the team from thinking we could win the league, to second to third top half please. But for this one I was hopeful. They do not know the way we play. Hoof and run. So I primed the boys – play our usual game – hard defence, get rid and hoof up front to our gazelle like striker. In the first minute we had scored – amazing! It was a fantastic game. From the start on a cold windy December morning we were up for it from the start. Our third keeper made some fantastic one on one saves and our striker chased everything and put them under pressure. We took the lead three times with them equalising twice. Great game but I fear for the return fixture. Their coach was not happy and most teams work out once they play us how to beat us - just man mark our striker and we don't have a plan B. Well we do it is other players score but that doesn't seem to work.

However, competitiveness aside what I really enjoy, once all the training and bickering is done, is getting the players on to the pitch and watching an evenly sided game against two respectful teams and managers on a sunny day in the countryside. That is one of the best moments as a coach. Sometimes I just look around and all is right with the world – until some fool tries to play out of defence!

CHAPTER TEN
TOURNAMENTS

I went to a tournament once. Where weaker teams are cannon fodder for the top teams so they can go on and win more trophies as well as their league trophies. No thank you. Once was enough as we got accosted by the car park attendant that charged us for parking and a paper leaflet. We wandered around a field, tried to warm up on a square metre of grass and proceed to get knocked out of the group stage without scoring a goal. And we paid for the privilege.

So sitting at one of our junior team meetings with the accountant haranguing us for not getting enough funds for that flood lit artificial ground that would make his life worth living and sarcastically pointing out that only three people have signed up to the astroturf lotto (the chairman, the accountant and the junior chairman) and I think it is a good idea to ask why don't we do a tournament. There is instant silence in the room and the other managers back away as you can audible hear the intake of breath and I suddenly realise I have not engaged my brain with my mouth.

"Are you volunteering then?" Those dreaded words. And off the accountant goes on how only him and one or two others (whom let's face it he allows to help – the chairman and the junior chairman) actually do all the work and how no one absolutely no one volunteers to do anything. Ok then – I rope in the newest manager, Bob, who seems keen – well he did bring his laptop to one of the meetings – so that has to count for something and brazen it out. "We'll do a tournament" I'm learning from the chairman and rope others in – we have formed a break away subcommittee of volunteers.

The three of us – Pete, Bob and me, in fine tradition, meet down the pub and bemoan how we got into this (I fail to mention because I volunteered them). In our FA coaching manual there is a section on how to run a tournament. I ignore it.

We decide a date – business sorted we update our progress to the junior team meeting. (I decide on the format of one meeting one decision – worked well for me in India – one decision a day, come to think about it works well in the library too). Anyway, date clashes with cricket, we re-arrange. This later clashes with the re-seeding of the pitches and for the tournament all the pitches have to be marked out in angles to protect the goal mouths and cricket square. We find out that the chairman, accountant and junior chairman are also in the cricket committee, the senior football committee and have a cricket and senior agenda (and a tennis one and no doubt in time a bowls one). This goes to explaining why the juniors play on the swamp and slope and the seniors on the new level playing fields. Don't even get me started on the facilities and the uncollected subs from the seniors...

Date sorted we advertise and I volunteer to be the contact person with Bob. Who somehow manages to get his name off the fliers. Managers start ringing and booking. I design a spreadsheet, booking forms and tournament rules. Thank god the library is quiet this time of the year. OK time for another sub-committee meeting. We would like representatives of each age group to attend but it's only me Bob and Pete. We begin to empathise with the chairman, accountant and junior chairman. We get invited to the chairman's house to discuss the catering, program design and general running of the day. The house is on the millionaire row of the village and has been built and designed by him. We must be taken seriously to get invited there. I completely ignore the fact that my house could fit in his kitchen and if need be we could hold the tournament in his garden. They rally round us and volunteer to help with the catering.

More teams are signing up. I work out a matrix and the number of pitches we need. I design a program and Bob gets the marketing sorted – he funnily enough gets sponsorship from the two pubs and says he has to do a lot of hospitality.

It's closing time

clean clean

emptees

Dave

look I'm serious. so shall I put you down [hic] for half a [hic] page? I'll pay half. Alright [hic] a full page half de price hic hic

BOB ON SPONSORSHIP DRIVE

Early on I decide I want this to be a "respect" tournament. All teams play equal games – scores are not kept and a trophy is awarded to the teams with the players, manager and coaches who show the most respect. This is decided by the referees. I want to encourage teams to play their "weaker" players and to encourage trying players in new positions and players to try their tricks. That is I want a fun atmosphere.

Needless to say I am not having fun as I realise we haven't enough goals, pitches, sponsors or volunteers. In time honoured management style I hold a meeting. I finalise the teams and pitches. We finalise the program and are ready to print. Two days later the girl's team, who haven't shown their faces for two months, insist they want a spot and bring two teams to the table. Frantic reworking of the pitches and programs and we go to print.

We borrow goals from another club and for our first respect tournament we have the senior players as referees. We decide to lay out the pitches the morning of the tournament. What could possible go wrong?

Time – time could go wrong as we don't have enough of it. Bob, Pete and myself turn up to set up seven pitches with goals, flags and respect barriers. None of the other managers show. Cursing like a sailor round the horn, I run around trying to set up. Teams start arriving and bless them help set up the pitches.

Dave

Frantic I look round for Bob to help but he has gone home to get his lawn mower. He has decided the grass is too long on two of the pitches and starts mowing them – with a sixteen inch wide lawn mower. After one length he has to empty the grass cuttings all the way over at the green container. It takes him ages and people come across just to watch him go up and down whilst around him the fields are like frantic ant hills. He was still mowing the pitch when the first game kicked off – mind you it did have a lovely strip pattern. One of our managers eventually turns up holding two of his kids and asks "Can I do anything to help?" He is offended when I say "Yes, you can set up the goals, put up the flags, set up the respect barriers, and oh yes sell some programs, flip burgers and direct the parking". Meanwhile Bob starts selling the programs, I go and welcome the teams in and where are the referees? Unbeknown to me there is an eighteenth birthday party the night before and a few seniors struggle in to ref looking like causalities from a zombie apocalypse film.

The chairman, accountant and junior chairman all turn up and help sell cakes and flip burgers. My player's parents have all baked cakes and we give them to the ladies running the café who have turned down all offers of help – despite being the loudest complainers of lack of help. The cakes are received like poison chalices. However all goes well and we stumble through the day. I walk miles chatting to everyone and talking to the visiting parents.

Finally the last trophy is handed out. I shake hands with the departing managers and everyone goes home. The ladies in the café return all the cakes my player's parents made. They didn't sell one. I realise there is nothing as queer as folk. I look around at the seven fully laid out pitches and me, Bob and Pete start to put all the goals, flags and respect barriers away into the green container. I collapse home at eight o clock happy with how the day has gone.

The tournament has proven a success and so I decide to continue to run one each year. I foolishly think that having done one it will get easier next time. Bob has complete delusions of grandeur and wants more teams, Pete ducks out having resigned as manager – hopefully nothing to do with being locked in the green container for two hours.

The following year I decide to invite the local FA to attend and to ask them to supply the referees. Unfortunately our senior referees didn't quite reflect the respect professionalism I had want to portray as those who turned up wore jeans and smelt of stale alcohol. In addition the FA promised a celebrity football player, their own trophies and an academy football squad to teach football skills. Unfortunately we believed them. Whilst the referees were excellent, we invited them separately to future tournaments, the FA failed to reach the height of their promises. It didn't bode well when they had a row with me about communication, mistaking me for the chairman because we had the same first name. Then their trophies were the size of egg cups and their celebrity football player couldn't turn up as there was an international match on at the same time as our tournament and he had gone to watch it – not play in it but watch it at home on the TV! Yes – maybe we could have done them for libel for the word "player". Anyway, fair dos they get someone in last minute. A mascot called the Kidderminster harrier. A sort of deranged chicken that looked like something the cat had brought it in the night before. But unexpectedly the children loved a giant stuffed chicken/ harrier and he was a hit at the trophy awards, despite reminding me of the puppeteer from Hi-De-Hi.

Each year the tournament gets a little bit bigger and each year my partner tries and gets me to refuse to do it. But unfortunately it is like a runaway train – with Bob driving manically shouting "We can get more teams, more pitches, make it bigger". However for all the money it brings I do think it would be easier for each manager to bung a hundred quid – but when it is all running and you look across at eight pitches of football and sixty teams coming to play and everyone is enjoying themselves playing football I think "job well done… I'll give it up next year".

CHAPTER ELEVEN
TACTICS

One would of course assume that there is a plan. Maybe not a cunning one but one that would take into account opposition play, team strengths, absentees, run of play that sort of thing. However you would be very sadly mistaken.

I see it on match of the day and marvel when they say things like "They must have practised this on the training ground" or "That was well worked" and think I am in some parallel universe. Is there another team out there that the coach explains a drill or a piece of set play, the players then listen, understand it and then practice it until they get it right? With my lot I am still at the "Please listen to me while I try and explain a drill" let alone "these are the finer points of football – if you defend out of position what happens?" I try to remove the hysteria from my voice as they shrug their shoulders and I avoid screaming "You get thrashed ten nil!"

So we started at the basics. As young players bees round a honey pot was our main approach to positional play, with the defence having a nice chat with our goalkeeper. So the first approach was to spread out – but of course that meant not having the ball all the time and so players had to avoid bunching up and tackling their own players.

This then brings in set positions. Remembering that the players have an attention span of a goldfish and that parents are shouting at their children to get the ball and not pass we quickly resembled a street brawl with one or two spectators.

Right lets go for a classic 3-3-2 formation. Don't even get me started on the premier line outs with 3-1-3-1-2 or 5-3-2-1. I went on a coach personal development training evening and was all fired up with a 3-2-1-2 line up and ideas of passing triangles and running off the ball. No chance. Back at the one hour training evening no one knew their position and we ended up clumped round the ball. No a classic easy formation. And then my defence turned into guards on sentry duty that patriotically stood on the six yard box and remained there throughout the game. "Move please move"

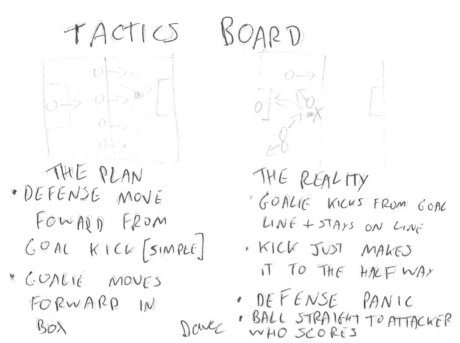

TACTICS BOARD

THE PLAN
• DEFENSE MOVE
   FOWARD FROM
   GOAL KICK [SIMPLE]
• GOALIE MOVES
   FORWARD IN
   BOX   Done

THE REALITY
• GOALIE KICKS FROM GOAL
   LINE + STAYS ON LINE
• KICK JUST MAKES
   IT TO THE HALF WAY
• DEFENSE PANIC
• BALL STRAIGHT TO ATTACKER
   WHO SCORES

But ok I can live with that – they have the basics – how about movement off the ball? Still we are attracted to the ball and if you start with all our team spread out at one end of the pitch I can guarantee by the time we have moved it to the other end there will be five players round the ball. It is made worse when we play other teams and they dink the ball round the pitch, as we end up in one brawling mass to play catch up. So for years we work on drills with play off the ball, I sit down and talk about positional play, marking, defending goal side. "What have we been working on?" "Passing" and come match time hoof the ball out, tackle each other and bunching up.

And all that is just positional play. And then one dark day the opposition coach in a corner to them told one of his players to stand in front of my goal keeper to put him off. All perfectly legal but eight year olds? Is it fair play? Am I naive? Completely impeded him and they score. So then not just the tactics of actual play but then tactics to set pieces. What to do when impeded, how many in a wall, runners off the ball? Who marks who?

So for a couple of drills it is set pieces – named players in the wall, set corner takers and penalty shooters and all this against the ethos of any player in any position. But goldfish need to know what they are doing, so this plan at least stops the arguments on the pitch.

So whilst there is a plan – positional responsibilities and set play this makes a huge assumption. We have enough to field a full squad. Before the match I work out the positions, the strength of the subs I am going to make and how that alters the balance. I play our weakest line out first and our strongest last in the hope that we hold out whilst we are fit and then when the opposition tire we bring on the strongest. Not quite like the wedding at Canaan more of a Lazarus approach. But it all goes peer shaped when ten minutes before the match the texts come in and so and so can't make it and I can barely manage a full squad. Cursing I often don't have time to call on Bob in the age group below us to ask for a few players. They don't have that one on match of the day "And what a brilliant move by Wenger to bring on the under 16s player to make a full squad – pity he spent the whole match running after the ball and tackling his own players"

Once in the game it is very much as Day-Lewis says "prove in the letting go" – my work is done and I sit back and watch the ensuing chaos. I do not bellow and scream at the side of the pitch – if I did – all the players would end up terrified to touch the ball and look to me every time they have the ball, and second, I want them to make the decisions and third I spend a lot of the time obsessively putting the footballs back in the bag in case other managers nick them. I am sure Bob nicks half of my kit when I'm not looking. So it is the inspiring half time talk – I try and think of Elizabeth the first

– "I might have a heart of a middle aged man" or Henry V "Once more into the breach" or even Churchill "so much owed to so few" but end up with a Delia "Come on! Where are you?!"

Sometimes when the game is already beyond us at half time I try and encourage them to see the second half as a new game

"Forget the first half – lets win this half" but I forget our players have a very literal view

"What? This is a new game?" "Doesn't the first half count then?"

"Yes, yes it does"

"So why doesn't it matter?"

Others join in "What? Are we playing two games?"

"No no, I was just saying lets focus on the second half"

"Is this a new game then?"

I have lost the initiative – we have a five minute break which is spent in an argument about whether we are playing one or two matches. I rally with a Delia cry as they meander back onto the pitch and try not to think about the Dunkirk spirit.

"Let's have 'em! Where are you!" And they meander back onto the pitch.

CHAPTER TWELVE
FUND RAISING

Along with my role as manager, coach, administrator, first aider, project coordinator, psychiatric nurse (yes there are a few managers I would happily section...), counsellor, baby sitter and general dog's body, I also have a role as fund raiser.

As though I haven't got enough on my plate without trying to tap the parents for more money. I mean ten times out of ten at the end of training or a match it is chaos, with everyone asking questions and the balls have disappeared and where are the bottles and don't forget away kit next week, am I really going to get the cash for our astro turf lotto. But no this is the accountant's life and he has dreams of an astro flood lit training ground. So every meeting it is a review of the subs and fund raising ideas. Seriously I am considering just paying not to do the tournament and have done with it. But no we try brain storming – Bob comes up with a vicars and

Nazis beer tent idea (see what I mean about psychiatric nurse) and has to be gently let down by the chairman.

For a year now the accountant has been pushing a monthly direct debit draw and tries to encourage everyone to join. It is met by down cast mumbles and so far only three people have join – and you know who they are! But the chairman likes Bob's party idea and we go for a Xmas party for the kids. Great, volunteers then – yes me and Bob and the chairman and the accountant volunteer. Fantastic – festive cheer just what we need.

Unfortunately we are all busy going to xmas parties in December so go for a date in November. Bob starts telling everyone I am going to dress up as Santa and I have to nip that one in the bud.

We decide on the village hall, booze for the parents and hot dogs for the kids. What else do we need…oh yes music.

This one seems pretty easy to organise, me and Bob on the door, Chairman on the bar and accountant's wife doing the dogs. As we get nearer I ask about the music – don't worry its sorted. So I let the parents know, who unaccountable seem enthused, full house then, for all the boys and girls team. As we are setting up, I still have a nagging doubt for the music and nag the chairman again who plonks a cassette radio player on the stage "sorted". In my stupidity I imagined a DJ or a dad or anyone organising the music – not a cassette of party music – this is "what I call music 14".

I notice the bar is stocked high – wise move- and head for the entrance to receive the guests. The venue is split into two – bar and dance hall. Which also evenly splits the age groups – parents bar and children dance hall.

Bob and I stay in the freezing entrance hall, preferring the cold than the dull beat and muffled screams of the dance hall. However I decide to venture forth – mainly for a beer and dog for Bob (apparently it is my round again) and enter the bar. Here the parents are seriously engaged in getting as much wine between them and reality as possible. Having discovered how cheap we are selling the booze compared to pubs some are on a mission. I check out the dance hall and have visions of Dante's hell crossed with Lord of the Flies crossed with St. Trinians. Little boys are running across the floor and throwing themselves to the ground skidding on their knees, there are close knit girls dancing with boys shoving into them. Other children are whirling round and round and sugar hyped kids bursting from the toilets soaked and screaming hysterically. I stagger back with Bob's dog and check my watch only half hour in – another two to go.

As the evening wears on Bob and I become some sort of reversed parallel universe bouncers. All the kids are trying to get out into the car park and Bob and I are trying to keep them in. The door to the toilets is just next to the exit so most of them go in there and there are screams and shrieks that makes the London dungeons sound like teletubby land. The sugar fixes start to kick in and the parents huddle in the bar – and I am reminded of a scene from Apocalypse Now – the one where there is all hell breaking loose outside and a small group of soldiers huddled inside a bunker not daring to move.

However, a long two hours later as we are mopping the village hall clean we decide what a success it has been and decide to do it again next year. We must of made five hundred pounds minus the float of course.

So each year we raise a few hundred and the odd thousand for the coffers and the subs are collect (or not if you are in the senior squads!) and then someone somewhere spends it on dug outs that blow over in the wind and we are back to square one.

CHAPTER THIRTEEN
VILLAGE POLITICS

I was so close. I so nearly made it into the inner circle. To be invited round to the chairman's house with the junior chairman and the accountant. To sit in his specifically designed giant house and kitchen. To meet up in the top pub, maybe to play golf and to go on day trips to Edgbaston, But no... I blew it.

It was going so well, for years I had been regularly attending club meetings, going to the league meetings. Even doing the pitch marking. And of course the tournaments. I have done three now and I was getting to be noticed by the other club managers and chairmen. So my pinnacle of achievement; I was asked to attend the posh football do. Basically a marque in a field with some chandeliers swinging in the wind whilst we all get drunk dancing to tapes of Bon Jovi. Normally I avoid this but having been asked to attend and being on the same table as Bob, who normally does attend these events (need I say more?), I turned up. Anyway it was a trophy event for the senior team but at the end I was awarded the village Bobby Robson cup for services to the club! Wow absolutely delighted. In the run up to giving the award the chairman did say I knew nothing about football, but let's let that go and enjoy the moment. The last time I won a cup was when I was eight and beat Justin Thomas in the junior sports day (ah heady days). Bob insisted I put the trophy on my head and posted it on Facebook but I didn't care. I was in! Or so I thought.

I should have seen the writing on the wall. Icarus flew too close to the sun, Caesar was stabbed in the back for being too powerful, King Lear was bought low by his pride.

For the past few years it was difficult to get the backing of the chairman to organise the tournament. There wasn't enough time, we need to give the grass a rest, it was too near to the cricket season (the main pitches are used by the cricket club in summer). So we did not do a tournament and still the committee moaned about doing everything and the lack of support.

And then parallel to this the cricket committee consisting of, you guessed it, the chairman, senior football chairman and the accountant; who have now also formed a sports committee, obtain funds to have a cricket pavilion built. The funding for this still remains a mystery as there were no cricket funds, and with the accountant no longer presenting a finance report of senior subs and outgoing expenses to the junior football committee, gossip is rife. But the pavilion goes up for the single adult cricket team and still the juniors are harangued about raising funds and getting our subs paid. I ask a few awkward questions that are brushed off and the meetings begin to dry up. We had one last year.

So with divisions appearing and with the junior committee having another agenda the new season starts.

Being the oldest junior age group we are allowed the privilege of playing on pitch one. We no longer play on the slope or swamp. But on the same pitch as the seniors but unfortunately the senior manager/ chairman considers it his personal pitch. Things go well to begin with but because there is no warm up areas other clubs assume they can warm up on the pitch. Most of the time I police this – it is drummed into us when we join the club "Don't warm up on the pitch" as well as "No one helps" and "Raise more money". Anyway we have a must win game and my concentration is taken with getting my boys settled and welcoming the referee.

As by magic the senior manager, Ian, is walking his dog and notices some of my players on the pitch. He starts screaming at me to get them off the pitch. As I do so, the away team arrive and go directly on the pitch down the other end to warm up. Ian goes ballistic and starts going a shade  of purple. I tell him to stop shouting at me and go and ask the opposition to warm up on elsewhere. I turn round and my keeper is now practising catching the ball from corners in the goal mouth. Ian is in a higher state of rage at this stage, as sort of a reverse of Buddha's enlightenment. However I tell him to stop "Yip yapping at me" and try and get on with my job. We lose this crucial game 2-1 and miss going top at the end of a season by one point.

You would have thought that would be it but no. Ian in a fit of self-righteous egotism writes to the junior chairman suggesting my team should play on the sloping pitch as I cannot show the respect he deserves. Oh my god. You could not make this up. Our chairman suggests I apologise and things are sort of patched up.

Unfortunately Ian is on patrol next week with his dog and before I get their some of my players are on the pitch. I usher them off as soon as I arrive with Ian looking daggers at me. So that is me out of the inner circle. But it gets worse.

With the chairman now distancing himself from the football club, the cricket team now becomes their latest project. The tournament is cancelled as it too near to the cricket season and the pitch markings might put off the cricket team! Pitch markings – not even dates clashing put a couple of fading white squares might confuse the cricket players who play in a large circle.

TROPHIES IN THE DARK

The fall from grace continues. We come second in the league and should get runners up trophies. But at the junior club presentation at the cricket clubhouse (no studs allowed inside- Ian is there with his dog to check) the chairman forgets to pick up our trophies and we are last on and everyone has gone home and the pavilion is in the dark (no lights). Our season ends with a whimper.

Surely things can get better as the season begins. But the fixtures come out and the pitch allocations are sent round. Pitch one is now only for the seniors and the juniors are allocated pitch two and the sloping pitch. So at one weekend pitch two has three matches on it with all staggered times whilst pitch one remains empty. Pitch two soon resembles the Somme and players need to be treated for trench foot. I query the pitch allocation but the chairman says we need to rest pitch one to allow the grass to grow. So we are relegated to pitch two where still the dugouts remain derelict two years after being blown down, after being built by a local builder – nudge nudge wink wink.

My fall from grace is complete. The status quo continues with no one helping, don't warm up on the pitches and raise more money and the pitch allocation comes out now sans senior squad.

CHAPTER FOURTEEN
ADMINISTRATION – A WEEK
IN THE LIFE OF A COACH

Whilst not quite a day in the life there is a routine and a tendency for punishment that at times makes a soviet work camp seem very familiar to the effort and work put in.

Sunday

Fill in the match form and put in the post to the league – or receive heavy fines and possibly solitary confinement. Write up the match report and send to Bob to upload on the website. I am the only coach who does this although how many times can you write "Played hard, shame we lost. Didn't deserve it. Might win next time"? Apparently twelve out of fifteen matches we play. We draw sometimes. Go on line and update the score for the referee. Always 80% as that is the number I can remember as it has to match the score card – which I have posted and forgotten the score I gave.

Monday

The chairman e-mails through pitch allocation. Now we have moved to eleven aside we have progressed from the swamp, to the slope, to the junior onto the senior pitches. This means we have to share the pitches so have either nine am or eleven am kick offs. Once I have the time I ring the away manager to confirm times. All times are set so these have to be negotiated i.e. "Sorry that's the time we have been given – nothing I can do about it"

Tuesday

E-mail the parents to confirm training times, to confirm match times (and place and lifts if away) and any other issues. This could range to reminders about subs (every e-mail), sizes and payments for training kit (beginning of season only), Christmas disco (oh the horror) and who left what kit/ water bottle etc at the last match (yes – every e-mail).

Wednesday

I then wait for the replies of who can and can't come to training and the match. I prepare the kit for the training. Empty water bottles and pump footballs. I consider drills and go over a few I might try. I then contact the referee to confirm time and place of match. Generally I try and do this from Monday onwards as we get fined if later than Wednesday but I try not to leave a message and speak to the ref direct.

Thursday

Training from six pm to seven pm. Although I get there fifteen minutes early to set up. Hump the goals out of the green container and wait for who turns up. One or two parents tell me whether their sons can make the training but as normal I have anything from six to fifteen boys. This makes in nigh on impossible to prepare and is one of the many gripes I have with the FA coach training. Please can you help us train half a dozen mix skilled kids rather than practice on eighteen attentive adults? I used to train on Fridays but the kids were so demob happy from finishing school that they could not concentrate and I spent the whole time trying to get the footballs off them.

That is one thing I have learnt – control the footballs. If you let them help themselves to the ball bag you have lost them for twenty minutes. To get the boys focus back you can try to count down from ten to get the footballs back – "You have ten seconds to put the balls back

- 10 – 9 - [kids kicking the ball as hard as they can anywhere]

– 8– "this is your time we are wasting"

- 7 -[one or two might glance at you]

- 6 – "this is football time you are wasting – I was going to have a match" – [some come back – others still repeatingly shooting at an empty net – I wouldn't mind so much but they are missing]

– 5 – "Come on boys – let's focus"

– 4 – [general stampede to get back means balls shot at the players that are sitting] – "what did I say about shooting into a crowd" I glance at Alex – he sheepishly grins

– 3 – "Come on boys we need to focus"

– 2 – [always one kicking the ball]

– 1 – [he swaggers across – pleased with himself] "Right let's talk football"

Friday

From conversations Thursday and e-mails I get an idea of who is playing for Saturday. So sit down and arrange the team. All have equal time so it is a case of rotating subs so as not to weaken the team too much. And to play the boys in the position I think best.

Saturday

Turn up early to set up, greet the ref and make repairs to the nets as he sees fit. Welcome the opposition and ask them to warm up off the pitch. Paranoid about this now as I had one of the senior managers tear across the pitch to bellow at me to get 3 of my players off the pitch as they warm up whilst I was distractedly talking to the ref. We have got to protect the grass. I now have a twitch to look over my shoulder whenever I hear heavy breathing and footsteps – I call it the senior twitch. I have known one senior manager come over to a junior game and take the corner flags for his pitch. The juniors were playing at the time.

I then warm up the boys for half an hour – completely fretting when players don't turn up and have to ring the parents. Because I try to give all the players equal match time players not turning up completely messes my team sheet and I have to re-think the whole thing as all the players swarm round begging to go into striker. No one begs to go in defence – funny that. Team warmed up, all present and positions sorted I discuss tactics – defence to move up, goalkeeper to dive and strikers to run off the ball and not to tackle each other – we are ready to play.

Whistle blows – and the storm clouds gather.

CHAPTER FIFTEEN   A
YEAR IN A LIFE OF A COACH

June

I did it again! Not quite as bad as shaving all my hair off but nearly. I have volunteered to do level 2 FA coaching. In December it seemed like a fairly good idea. I had already done youth modules one and two so I only need to do one block of level two to qualify. Sounds so easy. The club need level two coaches to get chartership status; I get the credos over senior managers. Win win. So I sign up and destroy four months of my life in one go. Three weekends of teaching and sessions (not drills), eight match self-assessments, one assignment and two coach assessments at home with own squad.

It all goes wrong on the first day. I walk into the group that has known each other and bonded over eight months and the course tutor repeatedly points me out as new as I slink in the back. No introductions just straight in with an alpha male table and I realise immediately I am out of my depth. I had read up on the previous course work but things had change. Out are warm ups, all realistic sessions, player involvement and all technical.

However the one thing that remains the same is the pecking order. One coach recognises me as we had had a "bit of a set to" at a match. He had shouted at a referee and I had told him to calm down. All mild stuff but incidents that get coaches struck off my Christmas list (no coach has yet made that list but they might!). Rather than be apologetic he was quite brazen. I didn't know why until we had a training session. And yes the one thing that remained the same was the pecking order by football skill. And he was one of the better players and therefore enjoyed alpha status. Unfortunately in the keep me up warm ups I had managed 2 and established myself at the lower end. Oh alright – at the back of the queue round the corner and rummaging in the bins. It also didn't help that my fitness was well down as I had stopped running for a bit – dodgy knee and complete lethargy I think is the medical term. So I staggered round the sessions praying for them to end. I also realised that I was the oldest one there which threw me into complete despair. I had hit fifty this year and thought I could cope but oh no. No I decided to ignore my birthday apart from the meal with family and the compulsory row with teenage hell children and the hissed "discussion" cross the table about mobile phone expenditure and the knife glares from the love of my life. Rather good value for Tesco vouchers I thought.

So after the first day of level two, confidence rock bottom and unable to move my legs I go for the "sod it" approach. Volunteer for all the sessions. I don't think I am learning here. So end up designing a session and told by the gleeful alphas on my table that I would have to deliver this next week and be filmed. I completely panicked, attempted to re-design the session, planned it in miniscule detail and had no sleep for a week. Only for the tutor to decide on something else for the weekend and I spent the whole weekend avoiding making suggestions and mentally giving myself a kicking on several levels of self-doubt and loathing. The last weekend is goalkeeping sessions and I have managed to avoid any deliveries and thank my lucky stars I have escaped relatively scot free as all the alphas arrange matches, congratulate each other and go for a kick about. The tutor mumbles something about a project and visits and I flee swearing never ever to volunteer again for these hell events. I am sure I saw Dante walk past last week and do a couple of keep me ups before heading in a blinder.

July

Right - the season was supposed to end in March but went into April because of all the terrible weather and the fact that our new pitches cannot cope with rain and needed to be protected for the seniors to play in the afternoon when miraculously the pitches had drained. So normally we had training sessions all June and then our trophy day early July where we would stop for a month or so. But because I had to analyse eight matches and had arranged a visit from the tutor late July I thought I'll keep on going. Oh bad bad mistake.

Trophy day was a fiasco as usual. So despite the junior managers wanting to make a bit of an event the chair was too busy to lead so in a last minute decision the half built cricket pavilion was to be used as a venue (in an attempt to justify spending all the football subs on it) and a barbecue and beer stall set up. All teams had allocated times and being the senior junior team we went last. No event for the children was organised – in the past I had done a tournament with all squad members but this had been vetoed in the past few years. So I turned up at seven o clock due on to give trophies at 7.45 to find feral kids all playing a mass football match whilst parents decided to take full advantage of the cheap beer stall. Each team over ran and by the time I was on it was dark and there was no electric in the pavilion. Also the chairman had forgotten to get our trophies for runners up in the league. This was a huge achievement for us and one I wanted to focus on. So on the steps of the cricket pavilion I hand the small trophies out from the club that Bob said looked like a sex toy, to a background of the last drunken parents as the bats swooped round us and I try and rally with a bang and not a whimper.

Miraculously our season was fantastic as we robbed nearly every team we played as we held firm and hoofed the ball down field to our cheetah like striker. Sometimes I felt like Dick Turpin. But it worked and I saw no reason to complicate things by having tactics. Play to our strengths: strong defence, hoof the ball up field, striker score – simple. But with nearly the last match to go we gave away a silly penalty and lost a vital game as they put eight behind the goal and we lost the season by a point. Oh well – the winning manager was never on my Christmas card list as he shouted at the ref., tried to intimidate our linesman and generally was one of those managers that you relish beating. So a bitter end to the season, but one in which I had wanted to try and raise the boys at the trophy day. But alas not to be.

So when the trophies were finally collected I arranged a parent (and sibling) and players match and handed them out then. One of the coaches had wanted a parent versus player match but after all the players started planning to "take me out" I decided it would be better if I refereed and I paired players up with their parents/siblings. We had a mixture of dads, mums, sisters and brothers playing and all was going well until our central midfielder got a bit carried away and took out Sarah from behind and we had to carry her off.

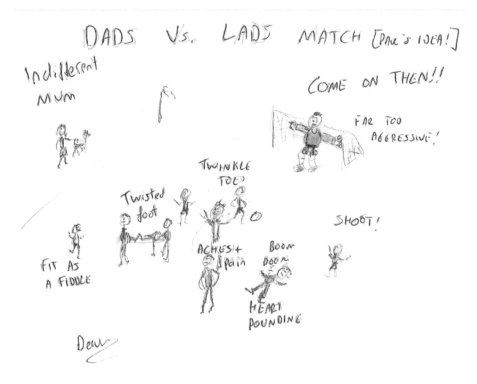

After the trophy day we continued to train and I arranged a few matches. I focused the training on mid-field shooting as for most of the season our midfield, defence and goal keeper all tried to kick the ball forward solely for our striker to bear down on goal like a train. I also wanted us to work on midfield going forward as they mainly thought their work was done once the hoof forward had been made and watched the game unfold in the penalty box from half way. In fact they tended to do that when we were defending too (that's this next year's session sorted – cover – or as explained from the touch line "GET BACK!!!).

So with renewed focus and enthusiasm after level two training I failed to anticipate the decline in motivation, concentration and attendance from my players as we moved into July and there were no competitive matches. I also had my assessment in late July – the only time the tutor could make, so I arranged a few friendlies and plugged on.

I also made the mistake of booking two tournaments. I had a deluded sense of our ability having ended up second (missing top by a point) in the league and thought "Oh we can win a trophy or two". I failed to even register the little self-doubt that tried to re-mind me the humiliation of the previous tournaments we had en-tered where we only scored one goal.

So all geared up with our top players in a five aside tournament we psychologically approach the seven minute matches like a long test match on a Sunday afternoon after a lunch of pie and mash and sponge and custard and meandered out. We were hit by a team resembling a sledge hammer on speed and got annihilated in the first of five games and come off outraged and shell shocked. The second we have a stab at closing players down but with no sense of urgency. Third game we raise ourselves as we played a team we have beaten but lose that. The fourth we go in with heads down and self-destruct and then the last one the penny drops and we play with some urgency. But to no avail. We lose all five matches and fail to score one goal – we do worse than the previous tournament two years ago and I regret booking us on another one the following week.

Needless to say the tournament does not go well. An eleven aside format three games spread over two hours plus I arrive an hour early it is hard to keep the boys motivated for ten minute games. The kick off times are changed and we have two hours to spare. The boys disappear and when we are due to go on I find them

outside

the hot dog stand having stuffed themselves. I think we are the only team that go on with sauce stains down our tops. I stick to the usual formation but we play with no enthusiasm or belief. We play teams we have never met before and our inability to string passes, to shoot and to defend is cruelly exposed. We do however score two goals and I deem the tournament a success as we quickly leave, secretly swearing never to enter another tournament again. But then maybe maybe the next one will be different. We could train for them that might help.

So back to training and faced with promotion next year I decided to have an optimistic approach and trained on the 5-3-2 and 5-4-1 formation. Complete and utter chaos as we not only lost to our local revivals in both the "friendlies", we had no sense of shape or match awareness and there was a mid-match rebellion as the team resorted back to 4-4-2. Oh well the day of the assessment was dawning and I had planned everything down in fine detail. I e-mailed the tutor who asked for my assignment and project work.

"I'm sorry?"

"Your project, you know your philosophy, your player profiles?"

"Oh yes of course (Oh no what the hell is he talking about!!!) "Yep all ready for you when I see you next week"

The tutor had mumbled something about a project but I thought it was just an eight match assessment. On frantically leafing through the level 2 book it mentions some things you *might* want to add to your project and the psychopathic, non-communicating tutor wants them all!! Thank god I am a pedantic librarian. Two days later, a lot of poetic licence and my weekend gone, I have a reasonable project that Milton would have been proud of – "justifying the ways of coach to the man"

The day comes for the assessment. I am fully prepared- the boys are told on pain of death not to be their usual selves, parents primed to be supportive (ie not there) and my assistant coaches (parent helpers that turn up in football gear and go straight in goal shoving our goalie to one side as they relive a very distant past) told to agree with everything I say.

I plan the drills meticulously motivated by the desire to get this out of the way so I can have some sleep from 4am onwards. I plan the warm up session, the session once warmed up, the main session and then the session game followed by the session warm down. I read up on the principles of play and learn quite a few things – like in defence the players close down an attacker rather than turn you back and duck when they look like shooting, mental note to self "could be useful". And I arrive an hour early to set up.

The assessor arrives and my parent helper immediately starts showing off and gets the late players to do press ups. I call him across to introduce him and he starts effing and blinding. I look on as though I have just entered the twilight zone and been beamed down into another body.

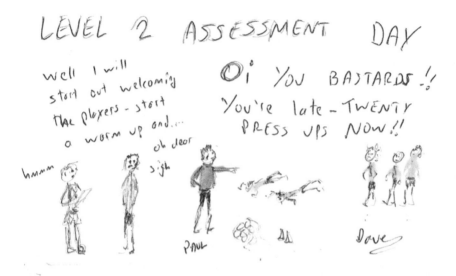

I get the pre-pre session underway and start coaching that, then the pre-session and then the coach stops me there and decides to "show" me a session. But it is identical to the one I was going to do. The boys all behave magnificently but it is the same as the one I was going to do. The twilight zone starts to implode and my confidence crumbles. As Paul is getting the boys to march round in the warm down I feebly end the session completely unsure whether I have passed or not. The coach runs off for another appointment, forgets my tome of a project and says he will be in contact. The parents who have been hiding in the dugout (I could see the fag smoke) rush across asking if I have passed. I bluff it "Of course"

The assessor rings and arranges to see me and the squad on the last training session before the season starts in September. Apparently level 2 is a process and the first meeting was only a bench mark. Glad to set the bar pretty low I look forward to a summer of anxiety. I finish off the season and rest from the year.

August

Throughout August I am harassed by managers wanting friendlies. They have rested all July and are gearing up for the new season. My nerve cracks two weeks into August (Bob has been training three times a week) and started their pre-season training. Two week rest in the year that mainly consists of poaching players from other teams and I sign up two and have one poached, whilst another leaves to do rowing. I am assured of the player's quality and once on the pitch I can see I was lied to. Oh no another doffus where I try and keep them out of harm's way. On the grapevine I hear of a team folding and all the best players going to our rivals. I start the training two steps back. I arrange two friendlies and decide on the training topic to be closing players down. I also make the decision to try not to make my level 2 over complicated. I go for a warm up, a session and then applied principles to a game. With the assessment our last training session before our first match I can't be mucking around and know from grim experience that after the summer holidays my defence and midfield would have put on half a stone each. They lumber into training and hoof the balls they could reach into orbit – oh well the July training of shooting is working – pity they haven't got out of our own defence before shooting.

Our pre-season friendlies go terribly wrong. I barely can manage eleven players and we get slaughtered. It is a cross between the Somme, an abattoir and platoon. Players limp off, I am on my knees and I forget the score (16-1 - something like that) as their manager kindly applies the latest euthanasia techniques and finishes the match with 5 minutes to go. At one stage our formation collapses and our centre forward asks who the centre forward is. I scream "You are!!" and the opposition managers chuckle.

I have a squad of fat hoofing kids – we're doomed

September

League P3 W1 D0 L2 F5 A9

Cup P1 W1 D0 L0 F6 A3

Two weeks to go before the first match. I focus on fitness and closing players down. The two new players fit in well in that they are unfit and sarcastic. I pore over the fixtures to see when the season ends – late March – oh well here goes.

The day of the second assessment comes round and I decide on a simple approach; warm ups, session and game. I get there early and find the girl's team have a fixture on the pitch (not allowed on the senior pitches) so have to set up on the swamp. I want to work on passing but the pitch is too small to begin with. So I have to change the session half way through which seems to delight the assessor. Momentarily I forget myself and shout at a few players but think I get away with it. I ask Paul to coach the goalies which he decides to do from the half way line but I decide the assessor has to find us as we are. We have to focus on the first match in two days' time. I don't even pre-empt the players with a warning. But for some strange reason I reach a state of calm – possibly my worried wearied body has surrendered. At the end the assessor gets everyone together and announces I have passed!! Absolute delight as I swear never to do a course again, although I did check about youth module 3 (apparently part of UEFA B – i.e. no chance) and relax. In your face senior managers – level 2!!

To celebrate we drastically lose to one of our rivals at the weekend. The first four matches all consist of playing teams that got promoted with us from group C so it all seems surreal. Evesham got promoted by default (one team cried wolf about promotion (our players have left) and stayed in group c [funnily enough they are doing rather well in the c league - strange that]. I do our old tactics of weak subs on first then slowly get stronger as I sub in thirds. Bad move. We conceded three goals in fifteen minutes and never recovered.

We play last year's winners of group C (who won by one bloody point) and in a bloody contest we beat them 3-2. Yes – we can aim for mid table. There is hope – that is quickly diminished when we play a genuine group B team and are given a hiding. We receive a formal complaint about one of our parents swearing at a player at the previous match from the league. I ask the parents what happened and one parent did confess he said "Calm down you sausage"

to a player who was fouling his son off the ball. I write a long official report and avoid anything that might be construed as sarcastic, rude, amused or bewildered. And genuinely condemn all unsporting behaviour at matches. To make matters worse we have them away in a weeks' time. However the complaint is not upheld and we get a reprimand.

With parents duly chastised and all the boys wanting to wear "You sausage" T-shirts we let our playing do the talking and we get spanked five one.

I can begin to sense the aura of calm despair – it is the hope that gets you.

I ring our local winter venue to book our usual Thursday evening slot as the nights begin to draw in and are told it has been booked to another team! What! These Thursday slots are gold dust and I spend a frantic three days ringing round venues to be only offered Friday slots at 9pm. I reluctantly accept an evening Monday slot at our old place with a promise of our old one back next year but am not happy about it. But decide to let it go and as my partner says "You get it out of the way quickly and can enjoy the rest of the week" Unfortunately she is spot on and then I worry about my motivation.

Bob tells me he plans to keep going until his squad get to u17s and I play another three years of football in my head – I don't tell my partner this but it seems to play out well. However Bob has four kids and seems to do a lot of things outside the house – his youngest has just started at the development squad which Bob now coaches, as well as his u14s and I see in his eyes the look of a man resigned to pushing a rock up a hill for eternity – well at least for another ten years.

October

League P1 W0 D0 L1 F1 A5

County cup P1 W0 D0 L1 F2 A7

Played three won one lost two we are mid table beginning of October! Wow. Having won a game I have reached our years objectives and try and encourage the boys. We have a cup match with a c team that we comfortably win. We look a different team when we are confident to pass the ball around and not just hoof it away. I try to encourage this at the next league match but we behave like frighten rabbits in the head lights when the ball comes to us – although a better simile would probably be like a driver throwing a spider off his lap in complete surprise, shock and fear and rolling his car off a cliff. The two midfielders decide their job is solely to defend, we remain in our own third of the pitch for most of the game and we occasionally send a ball up to the two lone strikers that have to take on the whole opposition as our midfielders decide half way line is far enough for me thank you very much. Miraculously they do score a goal and we come off 5-1 down.

We have a county cup match with an A team and I decide a 4-1-3-2 formation. I work hard at training with them on midfield passing but by the time Saturday comes their goldfish minds remember nothing. I am beginning to rue Monday nights training. However the first half we hold our own and come off with the score 2-1 down. We can do this. But Paul, whose son plays in defence, has been teaching him tactics – and the defence push up and try and play the offside trap. However they forget they are a stone over weight and only one of the players (Paul's son) knows about this tactic and we concede 3 or 4 goals in quick succession as their rather slow attacker out paces our even slower defence and scores one on one with our keeper who has a complete confidence melt down and has to be subbed with our third goalkeeper. However this seems to rally the squad and for the last quarter we dominate and score a beautiful goal that I have been working on for half the year. Our heavily marked striker takes the ball on the eighteen yard box, he lays it off for the oncoming central midfielder. The striker then makes a run left taking two defenders, the field opens up for the central midfielder to strike the ball like a rocket into the top right hand corner – seven two!! We come off slightly more buoyed than a dinghy at the end of a summer party and I realise we have a lot of work to do. I had planned to rest over the half term but plan extra training sessions and make a mental note to arrange some go karting or something before Christmas. We need to get the self believe and fun back. But mostly we need to get Jack back – our mega fit sweeper defence. He made an appearance at our last training session and the whole squad spontaneously clapped him as he entered the hall. Some players are just a talisman and I think we need him more than ever.

Half the squad turn up for the extra training (always the ones that don't need it) at half term and we take on Bob's squad in an impromptu friendly. We manage to win that one but the players have no belief and all the pressure falls on our striker. Paul suggests calling our strikers forwards so as not to put pressure on them. By the same logic I momently think of calling our defenders strollers but decide against it and grimly try to coach set pieces as the players throw mud at each other.

November

League P2 W1 D0 L1 F4 A5

Cup P1 W0 D0 L1 F0 A8

Friendly P1 W0 D0 L1 F2 A3

We have a bottom of the league match which is a must win for us both. A late kick off and the venue is over an hour's drive away. I load up the car with players and resemble the Ant Hill mob as we motor into the Cotswold. I revert back to a 4-4-2 formation and try not to sound too desperate in the team talk. We absorb some early pressure but we concede a stupid goal when from a corner our keeper catches the ball. Drops it and it rolls over the line as everyone looks on and no one not even their strikers reacts. I turn away and curse the pagan gods in the Rollrights. However we meander up to the other end the ball pings out of the eighteen yard box and our midfielder wallops it into the top corner seconds before half time. Second half and we play with a little self-belief. On the break we score a classic goal. Ball over the top, our striker latches onto it, one on one with the keeper and with a delicate chip we are 2-1 up!! The other team start turning the screw but we are used to this. All last season we absorbed the pressure and hit teams on the break. Solid strong defence and kicking the ball out – we hold firm. And then miracle of miracles with a corner our defence push up, it pings out again and one of our defenders volleys it in. Beautiful! 3-1 up and we might win it. I keep asking Tom the time 25 minutes to go! They

THE ROLLRIGHTS

PLEASE JUST ONCE - WE TOTALLY THRASH A TEAM !!

are all over us. 22 minutes to go. I know if we concede we will fall apart – we are still playing without belief. 20 minutes to go. Our defenders try to play the ball out with some fancy back heels and I nearly die as our goalkeeper makes some crucial saves. 18 minutes to go. Why are these games so long? One of the opposition players tries to rally his team but his voice hasn't broken. He shrilly shouts

"Come on! We can get one back!" in a piping voice. Two of our players reply in booming fog boat voices "First to the ball Lads! First to the ball!" We hold on and win. We go mid table. I go and visit the Rollright stones on the way back – thanks Cernunnos – I didn't mean what I said earlier!

But in typical god hubris we are drawn against the top team of pool A in the cup. Fraser was right "We are doomed". At training we work on 5-4-1 formation but the hall is so small we are bunched up and the boys just wallop the ball as hard as they can forgetting that we are working on passing. I say "forgetting" to try to ease the self-doubt in my coaching ability. A better word would be ignore. Paul tries to work with fitness with them but as they queue he goes in great lengths explaining the drill and the boys start fighting waiting to do the circuit. Thankful no one has been hit full in the face with the ball yet so I end training and try to get them to remember the basics – close players down!!

We are allocated the seniors pitch at home for the match but there was some rain the night before so in order to protect the pitch (for the seniors later in the afternoon) we are shoved onto the sloping pitch.

At least we can warm up on the pitch but as the game progresses it very quickly turns in to a muddy slippery pitch. Fantastic – suits our style of hoof and rob. We hold our own for twenty minutes and we get a penalty. I start to believe but the penalty is straight at the tiny wisp of a keeper. This annoys the opposition and they play the ball forward beautifully beating the offside trap and we concede. I sub our midfielder who turns out to be more influential than I thought and we concede 3 more goals before half time.

Belief is gone and we go one in the second half dead men walking. But again we hold on and keep them at bay but their finishing is clinical. We leave the pitch 8-0. The worse result I have ever had in a competitive game in eight years. I am gutted. The players are more interested in the biscuits that one of the parents brings rather than my debrief. I pick up the litter, the empty packets, bottles and loose footballs and drudge across the muddy pitch the drizzle and mud reflecting my mood.

I later arrange a friendly with a pool c team next weekend that fancy their chances and decide to vent my vengeance and terrible wrath on them and swear to smite them down.

Training is terrible and in a small hall the concentration and focus would make a gnat blush with shame. Being talked over, not paying attention and back chat are common. Paul nearly walks out and I decide on quick training drills and split the talkers up. I am unable to discuss tactics and some of the more able players are getting frustrated. I opt to chat to the boys individually and they all promise to be more focused. Yeah right.

The parents decide that as we have a friendly they can have a weekend off so we are down to eleven players. Over confident I play a 3-5-2 as we are down our main defenders and wrongly think our wing backs will actual play as wing backs. This is supposed to be morale boosting win but ends up in a morale sapping loss. The away team is more psychologically up for the game and wish to make a point as we "acquired" two of their players at the beginning of the season. One of whom scores a spectacular goal , dribbling the ball from centre eighteen yard box round three players, throwing in some step overs and from an acute angle, dinks the keeper. Probably the most satisfying moment of the season so far. We have another classic forward goal but he misses a bagful and his head starts to drop. They have six subs to our none and we just struggle in the last fifteen minutes and they score a scrambled goal mouth winner in the last few minutes. Just kick the bloody ball out! Their manager is delighted and wants a return match. I think we can handle that and I pray for full attendance and fitness.

Back to the league we have a winnable game at home. Not yet back on the haloed senior pitch one but on pitch two which is flat – joy!

We are minus two main defenders, a left midfielder and a forward – our captain that has more energy and commitment than a born again fire ball. We have half a sub as we welcome back Jake in his first competitive game for a third of a match.

We start the game feeling sorry for ourselves and forget to play football. We concede early on with a soft shot that dribbles through the keepers hands and then another with a dodgy penalty (aren't they all?). The boys begin to have personal battles on the pitch and the game turns ugly. We concede another from a good passing move. We forget how to do throw ins, we tackle each other and we forget positions. I despair and have my head in my hands for most of the first half.

At half time one of the players has to come off with an injury and we are down to ten players. I rollick them and "suggest" they play as part of a team. Second half we are all over them and score a fantastic goal – one on one with the keeper. They are desperate to get one back and start to argue amongst themselves – always a good sign. But their quality passing shows and as we tire we concede the fourth late in the game. I shout out "ten against eleven, ten against eleven come on boys" to make a point – reminds me of a few seasons ago when we rarely could put a full squad out and teams never matched our depleted squad despite their winning score line. Oh well, but we finish visibly buoyed and I wish we started the game like that. How do I get the players to believe in themselves?

Training on Monday again descends into horse play and there is a direct correlation between behaviour at training and performance on the pitch. Work to be done.

December

League P2 W0 D1 L1 F6 A7

First game of the month and I approach several parents to discuss training behaviour. One acknowledges his sons behaviour the other is more defensive and blames other players including my inconsistency. Apparently having a man of a match award and then being asked to behave at training gives double messages. Here's a single message for you "Your son mucks around because his parents ignore it!" Oh well I have the ace up my sleeve and have the poor behaviour at training means subbed for matches. Unfortunately I am beset by absences and injuries this month. This completely scuppers my plain for vengeance and I have to fill in both graves.

We play a team currently under achieving but in all encounters they have beaten us – including one memorable cup match where we were into fergie time plus when they scrapped an equaliser. So I think it is time for us to get a win.

Unfortunately my "defence" think otherwise and in the first five minutes we are 2 nil down and then concede another five minutes later. The first a weak shoot that bobbles past my keeper that he could have fallen on it but decides against this course of action and another who my star defender pulls a high ball down only to lay it perfectly for their incoming forwards to whack into the back of the net. I don't see the third as I am pacing up and down cursing this bunch of random players – not even a team. Twenty minutes in and three down. This is not going to go well.

However just before half time we get one back! My striker has been running around like a demented hare – closing players down, putting them under pressure and general looking like he wants to win. A lazy goal kick out and hesitating defender and he pounces on him and streaks at the goal – one on one – he has missed nearly all of these – I put my house on him missing and to my joy become homeless. Whistle goes, half time.

Team talk "At them" or words to that effect. We come out second half a different team and we close them down. Harry again plays a fabulous one two and we get another back! Do you believe? Yes I believe! But this annoys the other team and with some long balls put us under pressure as we push and our geriatric speeded defence fail to apply any pressure on a single forward and are too polite to make a tackle as he slots one past our keeper who comes out far too late. Four two game over. Or so I think. Our other striker Greg decides to play and give it a go and on a classic counter we get another one! Oh my god three four. The other team panics under pressure, we have believe and with minutes to go we scramble a goal in and it ends honours even. Fantastic in an understatement their manager says "he is not happy" but has the good grace to congratulate all our players. I am beaming. This is probably the best game I have seen us play in eight seasons. So delighted with the boys performance and character to get a result that I momently forgive all their behaviour at training and am on cloud nine for the weekend.

The weather plays a part in some postponed matches and we have a final match against a local rival to finish the year on. Four players out – we will have to fight for the bragging rights for this one. In the pre-arrangements their manager tries a few Mourhino tactics and claims they are playing so badly we will easily get the three points. Yeah right – he doesn't have three Christmas pudding defenders, Rudolph the cross legged midfielder and frosty the snowman striker. I have none of it and claim the underdog status.

I fire the team up with a Winston Churchill speech, this is the one, this is the game that keeps us up, this game defines us. Unfortunately we define ourselves as spineless goldfish that have forgotten all semblance of a team. We are a bunch of indifferent individuals and our midfielder under no pressure nonchalantly kicks the ball out for a corner.

From the subsequent corner the ball floats through our keepers hands who rather than catch it decided to pat it down to their unmarked striker to tap it in. I am incensed and pace the touch line and watch another ill defended attack that puts us two nil down. At half time I decide against throttling every single player and try and rally them. Cut out the hesitation, close

players down, push up. The talk seems to work and in the early stages we get a penalty. Straight at the keeper who then makes a brilliant double save as our striker actually follows up. In fact again, it is only two players on my side that look like they want to play. The striker and a defender that actual controls the ball, looks up and plays it. An individual goal and we get one back. Two one. However that annoys them and under the next attack we give them a goal. Our right back declines to make a tackle and our central defence fail to mark the runners' preferring to run towards the ball and a simple tap in puts the game beyond us. In the fading moments our striker scores and another but the game ends badly. Our midfielder is heavily tackled and he decides to push the opposition player – it looks ugly and the linesman runs on and pushes our player. The parents kick off and all descends into shouting and accusation. Our first yellow card – unsurprisingly from one of the ill-behaved players at training. The referee soon blows the whistle and my parents come over and want to complain – one about the shove the other for being called "Twat of the month". Both parents are the ones of the kids that muck about at training. So one official complaint later we do a "fun" training session and I just go through the motions – fitness, 5 aside tournaments and my Duke of Edinburgh student points out how disruptive those two players are to the squad. I know I know and I consider the dark side.

January

League P2 W0 D0 L2 F5 A10

Friendly P1 W0 D0 L1 F3 A5

Star Wars: The Return of the Jelly

Cast of Characters

DAFT RAIDER (age unknown, male), bad tempered commander of an elite galaxtic force

SITH PAUL (middle aged over weight alien), over eager second in command, waiting for his chance to take command. Has ridulous ideas

CHAIRMAN PALADINE (middle aged male), over stretched and over stressed lord of numerous elite forces

EMPORER JAR JAR WINKS (wrinkled old fossil) Over rules the entire force

GENERAL DEVIOUS (bespectacled nice gentleman), eaager and helpful, loyal to Darth Raider, second in command but due to retire

GENERAL BOB (middle aged, round alien), well versed in the dark arts, friend to Darth peer commander

SECRETARY BROWN OSE (Young female), loyal to Chairman Paladine and laughs at all his jokes (which are few).

Act 1 Scene 1

Daft Raider *and* **Sith Paul** *have received the battle command from* **Chairman Paladine.** *Their storm trooper 15B squad are to face the rebel alliance in the swamp sector. Whilst the senior elite squad will encounter the enemy on the pristine battlefields complete with pavilion for refreshments and dugouts for battle command to take shelter-* .**Daft Raider** *and* **Sith Paul** *shelter under a broken tree in a muddy field in the pouring rain as their troops begin to engage the enemy.*

Daft Raider: *All I'm saying is that it does not seem very fair, that's all.*

Sith Paul: *I'm right behind you mate. How can we battle in these conditions, what with the rain and mud? Command should support us more.*

(As if to emphasis his point a searing missile crashes into the storm troopers defence and they have to re-organise).

Daft Raider: *What was the defence doing? They didn't even close that attack down?*

Sith Paul: *We always start slowly mate, we'll get going in a bit don't worry*

(Another shot roars over the defences and the storm troopers scatter).

Daft Raider: *I'm sick of this- we have had two direct hits in five minutes. What's going on? We practised this on the training ground. Close your enemy down. It's basics. Oh no here they come again that's* *three direct hits!*

(**Daft Raider** *unleashes his light sabre and destroys a swamp rat in his fury. Sith Paul yells at the Stormtroopers to get organised. They look down hearted and as the rain gets heavier they regroup and trudge in for a debrief).*

Daft Raider: *Right lads we can do this. Keep it simple. Close the enemy down, make space to shoot and keep the shots in the air – the ground is a bog.*

(*The troops downwardly mutter their agreement and eagerly devour the chocolate and cocoa Sith Paul is handing out on a tray).*

HALF TIME MOTIVATION

Daft Raider: *Right now get back in there and show me what you have got!*

(*With renewed energy the Stormtroopers fight back and hit the enemy defences with two direct hits. But this enrages the rebels who counter and hit a crippling blow to the republic. The Stormtroopers make one last rally but the victory goes to the rebels and the Stormtroopers scat-*

ter away to their barracks).

Daft Raider and Sith Paul are left to put the defences away in the pouring rain and are heard muttering curses to the Stormtrooper guardians, the Stormtroopers and to Chairman Paladine

Act 1 Scene 2

Daft Raider *is on his death star in his office reading some papers. He picks one up reads it and sighs.*

*He activates his communicator and a hologram of **Chairman Paladine** appears:*

Chairman Paladine: *Yes what is it?*

Daft Raider: *erhm I have had some letters from the U15B squadron guardians and they are not very happy about the conditions of the battlefields...(Chairman Paladine is audibly heard taking a deep breath and the silence is cutting. Darth Raider continues)*

Daft Raider *erhm and the senior battle field was clear to use and they were wondering why we had to use the very muddy...*

Chairman Paladin cuts in

Chairman Paladine: *I am sick of the guardians, they should get up at 7.30 in the morning and f#cking line out the defences always complaining I'm sick of them..*

(The communication line goes dead and the hologram disappears).

Daft Raider sighs and makes an announcement on the telecom

Daft Raider: *Dear Guardians, I have spoken to the chairman and he feels he has equally shared out the battlefields and he is concerned of the drainage on the senior field and so tries to ensure battles take place evenly on the swamp. He also points out that other squads, particularly General Bob has solely battled on the swamp and they don't complain. So in light of our complaints we will continue to battle on the swamp. Thank you for your continued support.*

Act 2 Scene 1

To raise the troops moral **Sith Paul** *organises a raid on a lower rebel planet system. He reorganises the attacking formation and the surprise attack immediately makes three direct hits. However the rebels rally and as the battle continues five counter attacks prove decisive and the Stormtroopers retreat.*

He telecommunicates an update with Daft Raider who has gone home to look after his elderly father Daft Dad.

Daft Raider: *We were what?*

Sith Paul: *Erhm we had three direct hits to their none*

Daft Raider: *And what was the final damage account?*

Sith Paul: *Erhm, well I did do a new formation, and they started really quickly and I think they got a bit over confident and I might have got the replacements a bit wrong...*

Daft Raider cuts in

Daft Raider: *The final report was?*

Sith Paul: *Five hits to our three*

Daft Raider: *"F*cking hell (he imagines throttling Sith Paul)*

Sith Paul begins to choke

Daft Raider: *You have failed me for the last time Sith Paul*

Sith Paul: *Sorry mate I didn't hear that I was choking on a pretzel*

Daft Raider: *Oh nothing*

Act 2 Scene 2

Planet Eve Sham and the Senate announce their verdict on the guardian complaint of a adjudicator entering the field of battle and pushing a Stormtrooper in December. In a floral gown **Emperor Jar Jar Winks** *steps up*

Jar Jar Winks : *Hello hello is this thing on? Yes I have an announcement to make after careful consideration the Planet Eve Sham has a ruling on the complaint against Eve Sham battle squadron.*

We have decided to do nothing and that the guardian complaining is indeed "Twat of the month"

Thank you thank you. We take our responsibilities seriously and now we elect that we all forget this and move on

(The senate breaks into wild cheering and back slapping and retire to the bar).

Act 3 Scene 1

The galactic starship fleet heads off at light speed to the outer galaxy and come to a halt in a rural village solar system where the locals all look alike and have two heads, wear green wellies and kill anything living in the name of sport. The republic star fighters stare nervously out of the starships and four report to the sick bay immediately.

Daft Raider reverts to the squadron formation of two – four – four and **Sith Paul** is demoted to adjudicator. **General Devious** stands in next to Daft Raider in battle command looking out at the star fighters

Daft Raider :We have to win this battle if we are to stay in this quadrant. I do not want to go down to the lower sector. I can sense the force in this one.

General Devious: We have a strong battalion, we can destroy the rebels.

The star fighters fly out of the starships and engage with the rebel fleet. There is strong covering fire and support. Individual fighters call to each other and move forward as an unit. The rebels have no answer

Daft Raider: We must make this count. We have to strike the rebel base

But the rebels have two plucky individuals and their first attack surprises our defenders who cannot keep pace and the support vessel reacts too slowly and is hit, once, twice in quick succession in two attacks. We have time to regroup

Daft Raider: I can feel the force - we will strike back and we will strike back four times. This is our destiny. Trust me.

General Devious: Keep it the same, work quickly and the awards will come.

(But the storm clouds darken as the solar rain beats down, belief ebbs from the republic and the rebels sensing the force is with them push on and strike a further three times. The supply vessel is in flames and begins to crash to the sector below them. The fighters are lost and begin to disperse, but the remaining republic fleet somehow rally – they still fight on and hit two alliance supply ships and there is a small glimmer of hope that is soon snuffed out as the rebels strike again as our slow tug like fighters cannot keep pace with the streamline attacking force, all is lost and the depleted fleet limp home).

In the debrief the fighters lie on the ground or huddle together down hearted.

Daft Raider: *The force was strong with that one. We must find the plans to rebuild ourselves another death star like last year and then we can destroy all those before us. We must plan for the future, we must gather our forces we must...*

(Sith Paul turns up in a pinny and with a tray of drinks)

Sith Paul: Hot chocolate anyone?

(All the fighters rush over and grab drinks and chocolates).

Daft Raider: *Oh whats the bloody point?*

Act 3 Scene 2

Daft Raider *and* **Sith Paul** *are sitting on two camping chairs in the pouring rain beside a completely sodden field. It is almost dark with the heavy rain clouds. Sith Paul holds an umbrella up in an attempt to keep the rain off them both but it seems to channel the rain on to Daft Raider.*

Daft Raider: *Well I think the chairman has declared all battles off and we are to rest the battlefields. I might as well cancel battle drill.*

Sith Paul: *Oh don't do that I could always hire the ground at astro space. Me and drone Paul are going to do extra practice and I am sure the lads need the extra training and...*

Daft Raider: *No no I think it best I cancel*

Sith Paul: *Oh well, I have spoken to some of the guardians and they* *said extra training will...*

Daft Raider: *No no I'll send a communication out we can't fight in this*

(Daft Raider stands up and strides across the field he slips a couple of times but manages not to fall. He glances back and Sith Paul is doing a few keep me ups with a blaster).

Daft Raider: *Bastard*

Act 4 Scene 1

Daft Raider *and* **General Bob** *are in the canteen having a sonic juice discussing their battalion progress*

General Bob: *I couldn't believe the language the rebels were using, I mean in the height of a battle to come out with calling my Stormtroopers "Effing swamp rats" and some of the guardians were encouraging this...*

Daft Raider: *Disgusting*

General Bob: *Well when we got a direct hit I just went ballistic I tell you*

Daft Raider: *Smashing, I bet they didn't like that?*

Suddenly over the loud speaker an announcement is made:

Chiarman Paladine: Attention! Attention! This is Chairman Paladine. We have not received full payment from the Stormtroopers guardians and I am going to name and shame each battalion leader who has outstanding payments. Can I please remind you these payments go to the new space pavilion that is not just for the generals, all Stormtroopers are allowed to look at the pavilion and contribute to the maintenance. This payment is vital for the generals to enjoy the pavilion with their friends in summer.

Those who have outstanding payments are:

General Bob, (Daft Raider sniggers and points at him) Head Pallis, Commander Titch, Sergeant Maverick, Obi Quiet, Commander Insidious and Little boy Crusher.

This is the worse payment EVER!!"

The speaker goes dead and there is silence in the canteen. Daft Raider springs up and does a little dance

Daft Raider: *I'm on the good boy list, I'm a good boy.*

There is another announcement

Secretary Brown Ose: *This is Secretary Brown Ose I just want to say regarding Chairman Paladine's announcement this is the worse payment EVER!"*

General Bob: *That's it I'm joining the rebels*

Daft Raider: *Sssssh you can't say that!*

<u>*Act 5 Scene 1*</u>

Daft Raider and **Sith Paul** are in a battle simulation hall where their Stormtrooper squadron are running in what seems a chaotic and random way firing off their blasters at anything that moves. The room is in darkness only lit by blaster fire and explosions. They are standing to one side having a chat.

Daft Raider: *I had this really weird dream last night*

Sith Paul: *Yeah? Rolls his eyes behind Daft Raider's back*

Daft Raider: *I was like this sort of coach, and I had these kids I had to train...its all a bit weird*

Sith Paul: *Yeah, go on. (Interested despite himself.)*

Daft Raider: *Anyway I was sort of their leader and I had to show them this sport thing with a ball but they were rubbish...*

Sith Paul: *No!*

Daft Raider: *Yes they couldn't do it and they were all complaining and I had to try and be nice to them and help and it was so strange*

Sith Paul: *Sounds awful*

Daft Raider: *Yeah I woke – (Daft Raider is momently distracted) – Concentrate and close the attacker down!! – yeah, anyway I woke in a cold sweat and felt awful all day*

Sith Paul: *Nightmare*

Daft Raider:*Yeah I would have blastered the little f#ckers*

February

League P1 W0 D0 L1 F2 A3

February was wet. Wet wet wet and we suffered with cancelled matches. Not so much ours but other team fixtures. February was the month of doom where we were due to play all the top teams. But they were also in cup matches and as these got cancelled and re-scheduled our matches got put off until April and now May. We did however get one match. A team unbeaten and second only because they had played less games. As sacrificial lambs we set off across the county and I duly got lost and pulled up in a car park next to an under eleven squad praying that this was the team. No we were playing further down against the tree giants that you could easily spot in the distance.

Right David and Goliath speech later we trudged out in the rain onto the pitch. After absentees and no shows we have two subs and a fairly strong squad but no defence options. However the game starts well – we don't concede in the first five minutes and the home team is pushing forward defending a very high line. We are used to this – defend deep and send the ball over the top. However we fail to close players down on the edge of the box and get punished. But we continue to play to our strengths and our strikers latch onto two hoofs and we go in half time 2 one up! I can't believe it. It is not as though we played well – it is like last year when we robbed teams. Maybe maybe…no no don't start that. Just play the same.

Our players begin to tire and I turn to our subs but one refuses to go on as he "can't be bothered" I am momently dumbfounded and walk away. I go back and say the team needs him and he just repeats what I say and agrees and still refuses to go on. Nothing I can do. I reshuffle the team but players are playing out of position. We concede soon after and then a quick speculative shot with the keeper wrong footed and the game slips from us. Our keeper has a great game and keeps us in it but tiredness and lack of subs does us. The final whistle goes and I am battling immense disappointment with stunned disbelief in how close we were from getting a result. We trudge back to the car – the rain still coming and I have to rein in my thoughts as I am giving a lift to the non-player who refused to go back on. He is another of those who muck about at training.

The training later on Monday eventually goes OK but not after I have to say that I do not expect to be given the finger by one of the players and calling out the non-player saying he can leave if he wants as he continues not to apply himself. He is one that I say has a French temperament as he only seems to play when he wants to and has left and returned to us several times. He has no parental support which borders on neglect and I try to give him as much encouragement as possible but really, there are times when you need to stand up. Oh well he is only a kid but I don't expect to see him next year.

We get another e-mail from the increasingly desperate and psychotic chairman. The e-mail starts well enough with pitch allocation but he then starts to lose it regard match cancellations, rain and pitch fitness. He rants about managers, parents and players wanting to play football and declares a rule that if anyone warms up on the pitches they will be relegated to the sloping pitch. Bob and I are very tempted to e-mail "Regard the chairman's e-mail worse pitches EVER" but decide life is too short and we are relegated to the sloping pitch anyway.

March

League P1 W0 D0 L1 F0 A6

The month winter decided to kick in and the chairman lost his nerve. We only managed to have one match this month due to the rain, the hint of rain and moisture in the air. And oh yes huge snow drifts. Scheduled for full fixtures each weekend the cancelled matches had knock on effects as we were playing teams with cup fixtures that were re-scheduled immediately and now my season extends into May. Some of the fixtures were re-scheduled for Easter but after some frantic negotiations that match is now mid-week in April. The chairman completely freaked by the conditions starts cancelling matches at the beginning of the week, which helps Bob as he re-locates his matches to the club down the road that have somehow escaped the biblical floods that the chairman predicts. In fact like some mad Noah Cassandra figure – yes you can do anything in a smock! – he declares all pitches waterlogged in some doom laden e-mail as though it is punishment from God for having such poor subs. I batten down the hatches and decide to deal with the ill-discipline in the club.

I approach one of the parents to have a quiet word and end up on a barrage of complaint, I'm singling his child out, he always gets this, he's not that bad, there are other misbehaved children and he's got better things to do than this. Later he sends me a long e-mail asking me to reassure the child he is not being singled out. Unfortunately he is being singled out as he is the only one that misbehaves at every training session.

I give him one last chance saying that I would like to see his behaviour improve if I am to resign him at the end of the season. I don't hold out much hope of this as at this training session he spends the time diving and rolling around on the floor play acting to the laughing spectators. I begin to start trying out new players as my "French" player no longer turns up as I dropped him from one game. His parents e-mail saying he can't play as they are going away. This is such an obvious lie (the boy goes to the same school as my son) I e-mail them and say he has lost focus…again (he has left and returned to us twice now) and is welcome if he wishes to play. Unfortunately it is an e-mail into the void. I had tried to include this player throughout the years as he has had no parental support and I thought a team game with his mates might help him. But he is of the age where he can make his own choices and decisions and besides I need to think of the new players and the rest of the squad.

With the disruptive children staying away training goes well and I actually talk tactics, transitional play and in-position skills. This sets me up with high hopes as we face middle of the table opposition – all winnable games. We can turn our season round yet!

Unfortunately I forgot to tell my players this. With players absent due to school play commitments, hopefully not learning the dying swan, I have to field a changed squad with players in new positions. With memories equal to gold fish this confuses the team and we are all over the place. Our only recognised strikers is marked out of the game and our defence have a moment (80 minutes) of confidence crisis. I look at the bench and consider bringing that on as it is more solid than our back four. We go through the motions, conceding early, middle and late and make our way home.

However I later learn a rival team has folded and whilst we lost to them twice, everyone else beat them and so as the points are re-worked we move off the bottom. Result!

April

League P2 W1 D0 L1 F6 A10

Waiting for Matchot

Cast of Characters

FRED (Old male), Dishevelled in an old coat, full of bitterness and longing

ERNIE (Slightly younger male), Also dishevelled and over weight but has an air of confidence and knowledge

LUCKY (Young man) dressed in a smart white suit. Optimistic and friendly

UNLUCKY (Old woman),dressed in dark and is pessimistic and depressed

<u>Act One</u>

Two tramps are sitting in a dug out. It is mid-afternoon, overcast with a light drizzle.

Fred: *He was due today, but I had a note from the chairman saying he could not make it due to the terrible weather.*

(They both look out under the dug out at the hint of sunshine in the distance)

Fred: *What to do?*

Ernie: *Good question. How do we lead our life's? Do we follow a moral code or keep to the letter of the law? Are we positive or negative?*

Fred: *No no no what shall we do? He's not arrived yet and I have only seen him once a month so far*

Ernie: *Oh you mean Matchot? I think we should keep a tight back four,* *retain possession in midfield and...*

Fred: *Yes yes yes I know that but how do we do it? I mean he isn't even here yet and no one turns up for his pre-meetings and when they do they just muck about. Maybe it's me...*

Ernie: *Well there is a school of thought that says all existence is in the mind, Tibetan Buddhism I think.*

Fred: *I hate this waiting. How can you get going? How can you get any motivation? If it isn't Matchot it his admin. team. Sending out memos, chasing registrations, payments and always rude.*

(Fred stands up and holds up a piece of paper and waves it in triumph)

Fred: *Look at this? Rude rude rude.*

Ernie has dozed off and is asleep. Fred turns round and sees Ernie asleep and sighs.

Fred: *It will be better when the sun comes out.*

Ernie *(waking): Let's go?*

Fred: *We can't. We're waiting for Matchot.*

Ernie: *Whose that?*

(He points to the distance where two figures are approaching. One is all dressed in black the other in white. Both wear gowns and grey wigs, although one has been back combed and looks wild. They are in deep conversation with the figure in black occasionally waving his arms in animation).

Ernie: *Hello. Who are you?*

Lucky (dressed in white) takes off his wig and bows.

Lucky: *I am lucky and this is my esteemed colleague Mr Unlucky, (who makes a slight begrudging nod to Ernie and Fred). Matchot has sent us.*

Fred: *Any news is he coming? Are we to see him at last?*

Unlucky: *We are to bring you news – I saw him last week, or was it the week before, I can't remember but I do know you will not be pleased*

Fred: *Why what happened? Did we have the gods blessing?*

Ernie: *Oh please there are no gods – nothing is independent and exists purely within its own right and nothing is eternal. In fact I don't exist..*

Fred: *I wish*

Lucky: *Quite a philosopher, next he will be saying all is suffering*

Ernie: Well actually..

Fred, Lucky and **Unlucky:** Shut up!

Unlucky: As I was saying, I saw Matchot. He was doing well, and actually winning the court case. Two philosophical points well made, but they bought in new solicitors and his frail defence crumbled. I had heard he had relied on his second lawyer but a peppering of wit and argument brought him to his knees as he cursed his meagre and unfit argument and could not stop nine points well made. Matchot had wanted to be recognised as a cohesive force, whose argument was well thought through, balanced and skilful. But despite one last rally the court ruled against him and he was left alone and dejected. It is a good thing you have not met him.

Ernie: Oh the injustice, is man not a rational being? Can he not see the slights?

Fred: Oh what to do? We must rally, we must stand firm

Lucky: And that is the happy news I bring, for I too have seen Matchot and he is a much recovered man. The case was adjourned until mid-week and Matchot recalls one of his finest defence solicitors and back to basics with his standard team. The judge was a friend and set penalties against him but they were turned aside and his defence team brought one point, nay another point forward until the opposition replied. It was on a knives edge, but Matchot's key attacker scored a hat-trick of points and the argument was won

Fred: Rejoice – at last for the stakeholders were reminding us of our last victory...November apparently.

Ernie: Ad victoribus spolia

Fred: Exactly he who dares wins

Lucky: Come we must go, there are other court cases that need us

Unlucky: I hear that an argument was disallowed and one of the lawyers sent home. I must go.

Lucky and Unlucky leave

Fred: Alone again. What to do?

Ernie: *To life my friend to life*

May

League P2 W0 D0 L2 F8 A15

May and the season continues. The chairman sends out one of his happiest e-mails declaring all matches are off the good pitches and have to be played on the sloping pitch due to the cricket season. We did manage one match last month on pitch 1 but I had to line it out half hour before kick off. I spent a fraught two days expecting angry e-mails as I had seriously wobbled on the funny curve on the eighteen yard box and spent an hour after the match trying to rub it out! Happy to be on the sloping pitch and away from the patrolling seniors in their new cricket den. Apparently after a cricket match it is the place to be for an alternative cheaper version of the pubs, and rocks late into the night. Bob is trying to get invited but not made it into the inner sanctum yet.

So after many phone-calls re-arranging mid-week features we have our penultimate game against a team that previously roughed us up and won 3-9. After one of our strongest performances and win last month I am optimistic. If we win the last two games we stay up. With a full squad we can take the game to this team. However my players have other ideas and one by one they ring in sick – oops busy. I am down to eleven players and one of those has ingrowing toe nails and the main striker (my son) damages his knee in training. I get him to ice it, have hot baths and rest – but he insists on going out with his mates and limps home Friday. I tear my hair out and his mother shouts at me. I retreat muttering to my team sheet and try and manage the damage limitation.

Match day and we do get a full eleven – the combined miracle of teenage sleep and parent nagging and my striker is fit – we turn up and the atmosphere is like chickens in a slaughter house hosting a fox convention. We are playing a team that has won the league cup and is going for top of the table. They bring in ringers from other leagues (all legally signed up to our league as well), have sixteen players and look a professional outfit. I try and rally us – play for pride, play for the team, just kick the ball out and no silly attempts at control on the box. Get back to our basics- get rid, long ball and run at the players.

All goes well for the first ten minutes – we resist the onslaught but ridiculous decision making costs us and the opposition put away their chances. Our keeper decides against diving, our defenders don't bother to close the attackers down and turn away, whilst our midfield watch the game as they walk back, meanwhile our striker (the other one not my son [managers award of the year coming up!]) continues to stand off-side and is blown offside when we manage to connect to the ball and kick it up midfield.

However we manage to get one on the break and when we do attack they look vulnerable. This does nothing to my mood as I rue the absentees. The player with the ingrowing toenail comes off with blisters and we are down to ten. Of course they don't change their squad size despite the game being over score wise, but we continue to push and actually get one back. I am delighted for the players and we go in half time 2 – 5 down. Wow.

An inspiring half time talk and the ten players go on geared up and we immediately concede. The onslaught is predictable and I try and shout encouragement. The worse moment is when they are 9-3 up and in the final minutes the referee awards them a fifty fifty penalty. They give it to one of their smallest players as he has obviously not scored before. But it is a weak penalty, our keeper actually saves it – as it is straight at him so no need to dive, but he is so surprised by it he spills, our players already expecting him to score, don't follow up so the striker has an easy tap in following up. The cheers are hysterical and I look on with despair in my heart.

This bloody season could have been so different. I have 4 or 5 that want to play, 8 or 10 that want to be with their mates and the rest that just muck around. Saying that, the ingrowing toe kid goes back on and adds some spirit to the deflated team but we trudge off and put this game behind us. The opposition manager is impressed we put 6 past them in total but we conceded 19. Not good enough. Our defence is too weak this season.

We have one last home game left against the bottom team. We are both relegated and a result either way won't change our final position. So with nothing to loss or gain we arrange a mid-week game and all but one of my players is available. The hope creeps in as we have beaten this team before and I want to win for the lads to end the season on the high, nothing to do with my competitive side at all...honest.

I am actually in a good mood and chat amiably with the opposition manager and players. But as soon as the game starts they completely go in for the kill. Players are hacked and shoved all over the place. I look to the referee but he is oblivious to it. Worse is that the ground is hard and the ball bounces unexpectedly high so heads and feet go in and it is carnage. But I have prepped the squad to play to our strengths, long ball no nonsense defending. It pays off and we score two quick goals to take the lead. The opposition start arguing amongst themselves and I begin to feel optimistic. However the fouling gets worse and our players begin to shove back. A one and one with the keeper which the keeper gets to first is deemed as a penalty and a shoulder barge also a penalty. We concede both and the score is level. Things get ridiculous when my striker is brought down in the box one on one and I have to carry him off – nothing given. The game begins to slip as players begin to feel they can just dive in and one opposition player nearly pole axes a defender. But the game goes on and another breakaway goal for us sees us go in 3 – 2 up at half time. However an end of a season game, of two bottom teams whose result doesn't affect the standings, has a very nasty feel to it and we try to help the boys keep focused on the football. Our linesman is fuming about our striker being brought down and complains to the referee but he says he did not see it, he politely suggests that he then might consult the linesman. We go back on but our heart isn't in it – we concede three further goals to go down 3-5. There is a drinks break and I rally them; "This is our last fifteen minutes of the season, let's play as you want to, no fear – get out there!" It actually works. Our winger is having a blinder, they concede a corner, he losses his marker and headers in a powerful goal. He is all pumped up and punches his badge. He plays a lovely cross that comes out to him as he is running in and he half volleys an equaliser with minutes to go. We go ballistic and I generously think that is a fair result, but our defensive frailties of all season haunt us. Their bad boy player that has received a yellow card for fouling and diving picks up the ball on our box. We fail to close him down and he shoots. Our keeper stretches a hand out instead of diving and it goes in.

NON - DIVING KEEPER

We lose 6-5. Story of our season. Spirited attack let down by indifferent defending. We are all deflated and fired up against the ref at the same time. The whistle blows and we trudge off. Admittedly one of the most exciting games of the season, three penalties, one yellow, eleven goals and a game that could have gone either way. I buck the boys up and give man of the match to our winger.

All statistics for the year

Played	Won	Draw	Lost	For	Against
League:					
16	3	1	12	37	70
League cup:					
2	1	0	1	8	10
County Cup:					
1	0	0	1	2	7
Friendlies:					
2	0	0	2	5	8
Total:					
21	4	1	16	52	95

We have one more match with parents and siblings arranged, the trophy presentation and an end of the season treat left.

The parent match is where we pair up parents and players rather than set up direct competition and family strife. We all do the warm ups and I ref. Players and parents vote with their feet and we manage to have 9 aside. I kick Bob off down the other end of the pitch whose season strangely mirrors mine for the same age group and he finishes second in the table. However he was not leading for the whole season before an unexpected loss to a bottom team whose manage fist pumps the air when he realised that loss cost us the title. Oh yes we play them next season as we go down. In fact we have several grudge teams.

1)   That team that cost us the title and the manager then fist pumped the air. Nothing but complete annihilation will do and I want us to hammer their goal, smashing in a goal every minute and seeing their manager crying in despair

2)   Another lower division team where the only parent that didn't pay their subs and then complained to me when I wanted the kit back scurried off to. We played them last season in a friendly to boost our confidence but they beat us much to the delight of "Mick" who helps them out now. Again complete annihilation is expected and demanded

3)   And finally that dirty team that beat us at the end of the season. Just two comfortable wins will do and the team imploding in bitter recrimination.

So six games that I will be pouring over the fixture lists and demanding all players are fit and subbing the weaklings. Gloves off!

Anyway back to our friendly parents and players match and no parent is carried off the pitch unlike last year. Mainly as only one parent (new player) is stupid enough to volunteer to play. He does however manage to kick the ball fully into his son's tender parts who doubles up on the floor in agony and we all cheer. Nothing like team spirit. Paul goes in goal for a penalty shoot-out and performs his dying swan act. It is won by our defender who just boots the ball as hard as he can and Paul is too old and canny to break his fingers. Everyone happy we go to the pub. And somehow I agree to re-sign all the annoying kids for next season – strong stuff that orange juice and soda! There is reason in my madness; all the new kids that were going to sign up have cleared off and the feedback I am given is that I am a shit manager! Yes and you're point? So I re-sign most of my players as I need as many players as possible to field a full squad. Oh well – we lose two and sign up two – so honours even.

The trophy day arrives. The day I dread as I hand out the manager's award and see all the bitter look in sixteen parents eyes as I award someone who isn't their child and I stutteringly praise the child to the delight of one person. Oh well. Last year was a fiasco so Paul and I plan a world cup tournament for the players beforehand. Other age groups ask to join us as we are the only organised team and we are soon running a full tournament. Bob, having joined the dark side by joining the tennis and cricket club, has a prime spot and finishes early. However he blots his copy book as he has arranged for an ice cream van to come up to the cricket pavilion which is consequently chased off the pitch by the chairman, secretary and accountant to the background of greensleeves played at a slightly speeded version as it shots off. Unfortunately the kids all get excited and also chase the van as it disappears round the corner with the accountant last seen in his apron waving his spatula shouting about this year's profits for new cricket screens. As I walk past the marquee I over hear the secretaries husband at his presentation announce they have been promised all their matches on the sacred flat pitches and I realise we have another season on the sloping pitch. Oh well – nothing different there then. It is my time to come forward and hand out the trophies. We shuffle into a hot sweaty marquee that has been set up for the senior trophy and ball night. Juniors begrudgingly sent an invite a day before the event. So I begin:

"Thank you all for making the trophy presentation. I see from the size of them we are still paying off the cricket pavilion" pause – silence - I continue "Firstly I would like to thank the chairman for organising the club and team, without him we wouldn't be playing on the sloping pitch whilst he protects the good pitches for the seniors. Without his balls he ensures his friends play on the best pitches all season." There is an audible sharp intake of breath and I have their full attention. "I would also like to thank the secretary for sending us rude e-mails about the subs and generally backing up all the angry e-mails from the chairman. I would like to go on record and say I do not support any gossip or rumour about the chairman and secretary as it is obvious." There are a few embarrassed titters (no not my players).

"And then I would like to thank the parents. Without them there would be no matches as they ferry their children from place to place. I have found their whining and whinging particularly irritating this year and their inability to discipline their children is reflected by their child's behaviour on and off the pitch." Some of the parents start booing and stand up as if to leave.

I carry on – in for a penny "And finally I would like to thank the players, who have half-heartedly played, who muck about at training and who have been rude and obnoxious. We got the results we deserve this season as half of you couldn't be bothered and so we are relegated to play with the other hoofers – thanks lads for your none effort and wasting mine and Pauls time". I sarcastically give a slow clap. The parents are all standing up now and are shouting and jeering. I ignore them and start shouting

"And so we come to the trophies – well they all go to my son, who has more talent in his little finger than the rest of you put together. Right that's it for another season – clear off whilst I enjoy Saturday mornings and reclaim my life back from you bunch of ungrateful, talentless shits and that's just the parents!"

The parents all start shouting and tussle with Paul. A few chairs are thrown and an ostrich runs across the room, I start throwing ice cream dressed as an umpire, Bob is fighting with Paul and ….

The chairman shakes me from my day dream – "Hey you're due on next, we're waiting"

"Oops sorry" and with a bound I go up front and begin "Thank you all for making the trophy presentation" I pause and look at all the expectant faces of the parents, of the chairman and secretary lining out the trophies, the boys all sitting in their kit and I feel a rare surge of paternal pride and so continue "it has been a hard season…"

CHAPTER SIXTEEN   THE FINAL YEAR: NOT WITH A BANG BUT A WHIMPER

Well all change, the chairman resigns under rumour and counter rumour of inappropriate behaviour. And Tom my long standing parent helper decides to call it a day – fair do - his son had stopped playing last year.

So I ask Paul to take a more active role in helping and he immediately starts to row with everyone. At our winter training ground he rows with both teams either side of us – I try and point out we have until March to get along with them but he then goes off and argues with the administrators as one team has a half pitch and we have a quarter, despite this was our agreement.

He then argues with opposition managers and referees, as well as swearing and querying my substitute decisions, insisting that

we only play the strongest players and not rotate. It accumulates in him being told off by a referee as the ref overheard him being disparaging about some of his decisions. I have a long talk to him about my philosophy and approach. I also decide to call it a day – completely unrelated...honest, as we have reached the end of our youth age group. He wants to take the squad into the under eighteens league and I am happy for him to do so. He immediately starts calling the team his but I decide to let go a bit more and allow him to do so and he calms down a bit. He still has a mohawk, wears skin tight lycro shorts, has a builders bum and insists in warming up in goal with the players, but I try to take the role of mentor and am encouraged by his boundless enthusiasm. My son now has other focuses as he tries to work on his acting career and is missing more and more training sessions. Despite that his fitness is next to none and remains one of the few players that makes a difference on the pitch. The other game changer is our main defender, who was injured for most of last season and whom I now suspect has wanted to give up football but could not tell me. He now never turns up. Consequently this season we have really struggled to get a full squad together with me even getting Tom's son in (who has left) to boost numbers as we put out 10 against 11 (plus 5 subs) in one match - like the old days. In that match we lead twice but tiredness got to us as we lost that one 4-2. Can't wait for the re-match with a full squad – fingers crossed – yeah right my squad turned up for the re-match in body but not in spirit and we conceded two unmarked headers from set pieces and scored an own goal. The gods are cruel. In fact a lot of players dropped out at the start of the season and we have had sporadic attendance as the academic year gets underway. I am left with the dossers from last year and players with varied ability, with only one or two game changers. There are now very few from the original under eights – five but only two regularly turn up. And somehow I feel I have let the squad down as the atmosphere has changed into a more aggressive and competitive one. The players that left maybe were not the best ability but they were kind and hard working. However I feel I have a loyalty to the old squad members and determine to see the season out.

The other change is that somehow Bob has managed to take on the role of chairman! OMG wolf amongst the sheep. All those years in the cricket club has paid off! He takes to the role with zealous zeal and in our first managers meeting insist we fund raise by having a tournament (no longer a respect emphasis as we found out the seniors made £1400 by opening the bar in the pavilion on boxing day for a "friendly"), Bob also wants us to have a bonfire night and a christmas disco. I tentatively suggest taking the managers out for a thank you curry but he ignores me. I flash him a badge on the inside of my lapel I had made "Bring back Pete" (our old chairman) and he momently stutters as he starts naming and shaming the managers with the most outstanding subs. Same same but different. Neither the tournament or the disco happens as the former clashes with any cricket dates and the latter we can't book the village hall. For some reason all the dates we suggest are full – I wonder if they remember the last time?!

The village hall has now become the epicentre for our very own green goddess and at all hours desperate middle aged villagers can be seen being put through their paces by some militia fitness brown shirts as they struggle and gasp their way to fitness. I managed to escape after a year with only a damaged knee. Others have not been so lucky and have had to be stretched out to freedom. The last I heard the escape committee were working on a tunnel.

Being level 2 and having two youth development badges (thought I'll drop that in) and being the senior squad you would have thought the squad would be doing fairly well, couple of evenly matched games, no real upsets just a good competitive league. Yeah you would think that but for some insane reason the league has decided to enter all junior football teams into a county cup. So rather than play teams in your league (bottom) we are offered, like lambs, to teams within the county – so academy leagues, super league teams and plain good team leagues. And as the gods bring hubris they also bring the kidderminster harriers – you remember the team with the deranged mascot out of our respect tournament. But their league has been transformed and they play premiership youth squads and win!

So we are drawn with them in a home fixture – all on pitch one under the beady eye of the chairman (mad Bob), the accountant and patrolling senior managers (don't warm up on that pitch!!)

Alarms should have gone when the away manager asked me if there was a lunch provided. You what! I told him the accountants wife was frying half a pig in the cricket – oops football pavillion.

Anyway having warmed up on the sloping pitched – i.e. hoofing practice (we lost 2 balls...actually we lost a few more than that during the game) and our team watch the opposition warm up like some Ronaldo Madonnas with their THREE full time coaches we went off to play with as much enthusiasm as someone walking to the scaffold asked to give a dance.

Needless to say it was not pretty but what made it worse was their manager sent me across the match statistics...I have no reason why, maybe we would find them useful?

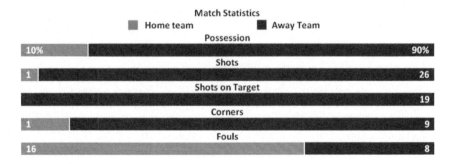

I don't!

They had also videoed the game so they could use it for training and their manager asked whether I wanted a copy. I declined but suspected they might just use the video for an entertainment night or make £250 sending it to "You've been framed".

To make matters worse was we actually used the cricket changing rooms in the pavilion – just to try and appear professional and I was so disheartened I asked our accountant to lock up the away changing rooms as I left before the harriers and an hour later I get a furious e-mail – apparently the harriers had left half a sandwich behind and it was my responsibility to pick it up. Can't win – literally.

The season rolls on and the grudges continue...really must try with the players. So far no cancelled matches and I am counting down.

Paul then stakes a fancy to one of the single mums and badgers that her son goes in strike. Sure we need a third striker so I play him a couple of times and he closes down all the defenders but can't shot or pass the ball. As Paul is effing and blinding at the side line I ruefully say "He can't shot for toffee". Unfortunately this gets back to his mum – bloody blabber mouth subs and she shouts at me that I have affected his confidence – Paul stands in the background smirking. However the infatuation soon ends and I am under less pressure to play him.

However I soon get into even more trouble. We are at home playing the league Chairman's team. Paul is swearing away and the chairman asks him to curb his language. As luck would have it one of my players shoves an opposing player into the metal fences protecting the hallowed cricket pitch and Paul rushes to the rescue. He throws the fences away from there one metre position from the pitch and then tries to alert the referee to a dog that has run on the pitch and done a poo. Meanwhile the opposing player, ignored by Paul is carried off. The game continues and Paul frantically waves to the referee pointing to the dog poo but all you can hear is Paul pointing at the referee shouting "Shit!"

He wisely decides to lurk at the cricket pavilion during the rest of the game chatting to the mums. This leaves me on my own next to three of the opposing managers. The match is ugly and they shout at the referee and challenge him all the time – which he soon becomes influenced by. This winds me up something chronic, particularly as my son is blatantly pole-axed in the box and the referee says he can't give it as he did not see it despite the linesman flagging wildly. My players are incensed and he begins handing out yellows as my players start swearing. I wonder where they get that from? We lose the game in one of the worse refereed matches I have seen. Paul slopes back and I ball him out saying he should have been in the dugout supporting the term rather than with his girlfriend. Big mistake. All hell breaks out when she hears my comment and apparently I am lucky her son doesn't deck me one. Apparently she has taught him that she can be friends with males without sleeping with them and I have undermined this valuable lesson. I don't know what to say so profusely apologise and look to the end of the season. Paul smirks in the background. I really begin to hate him.

In a miracle we have no postponed matches and the last game comes on the day I fly to India in the evening for a Buddhist retreat. I seriously need a couple of life times to purge myself from all the karma I have created. The last match is a grudge match at home on the sacred pitch one. I am desperate to end on a high...well just not to loss and play all my best players. Unfortunately that is normally the problem, but to add to my woes I only have eleven players.

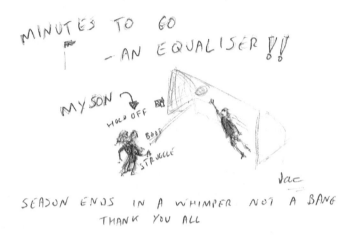

The other team are up for it and ours wilt from the start. We soon go two nil down and I bow to the inevitable. I try to rouse them from their stupor at half time. Bless him my son tries to rally the players but their minds are elsewhere. So he takes it upon himself and hounds down the ball. He chases a back pass and as the keeper fumbles under pressure he rounds him and slots home. Fantastic. He continues to single handedly take the game by the scruff of the next and headers a cross into the back of the net and we equalise with minutes to go. Our nerve starts to go and I desperately shout "Play the old way" "Play the old way!" Hoff it out and long to the strikers. We survive the pressure and the whistle goes. Two two – we didn't lose and my son scores a brace. I am beamingly so proud of him and hug him. Thank you son, thank you for so much fun [and not ending on a loss!

ABOUT THE AUTHOR

David Chamberlain

David has Level FA 1 in goalkeeping coaching, level FA 2 in football coaching and Modules 1 & 2 in FA Youth Development. He was a grassroots football coach and manager for 10 years and has spent the three previous years as a touchside parent for his oldest son.

He has two boys who still play football at University in a five aside team. They have not been  too badly psychologically scarred by their Dad screaming "Get rid!!".

However I still suffer flash backs after my oldest son decided in a cup game instead of tapping a rolling ball into an open goal to go on his hands and knees to head in the winning goal and misse!!. His team consequently lost the game.

I am pictured here awarded the club "Bobby Robson" cup. Finally a big piece of silverware!!

BOOKS BY THIS AUTHOR

A Walk With My Father

This book tells the story of Terry's life and his last years living with Dementia. Terry and his son navigate the difficult options and choices as he loses his home and is moved from nursing home to care home. Often alone and without any support Terry is taken advantaged of by friends and family and is pushed between services. With numerous hospital admissions and re-locations David weaves astories of Terry's life and memories of war torn London with practical advice on dealing with the hard decisions that they both faced. It is a story of love and reslience.

ACKNOWLEDGEMENT

I like to ackowledge Alison for putting up with all the stress and chaos, but who secretly enjoyed waving us off on Saturday mornings! To all the coaches and parent helpers and parents, in particular; Bill, Simon, Tim, Sal, Amanda, Paul and Rob.

To my two boys, Jack and Harry that gave me so much enjoyment seeing them play football with their mates.

A huge acknowledgement to David, our past junior chairman, that sponsored us twice for kit and supported the respect tournaments. Fantastic ethos and encouragement.

Also the FA in Worcestershire and the Evesham Ambassador leagues. Great league, great training and full of dedicated staff and volunteers.

And finally I acknowledge the children that played football for us and against us in the league and cups - we had so much fun...I hope!

Printed in Great Britain
by Amazon